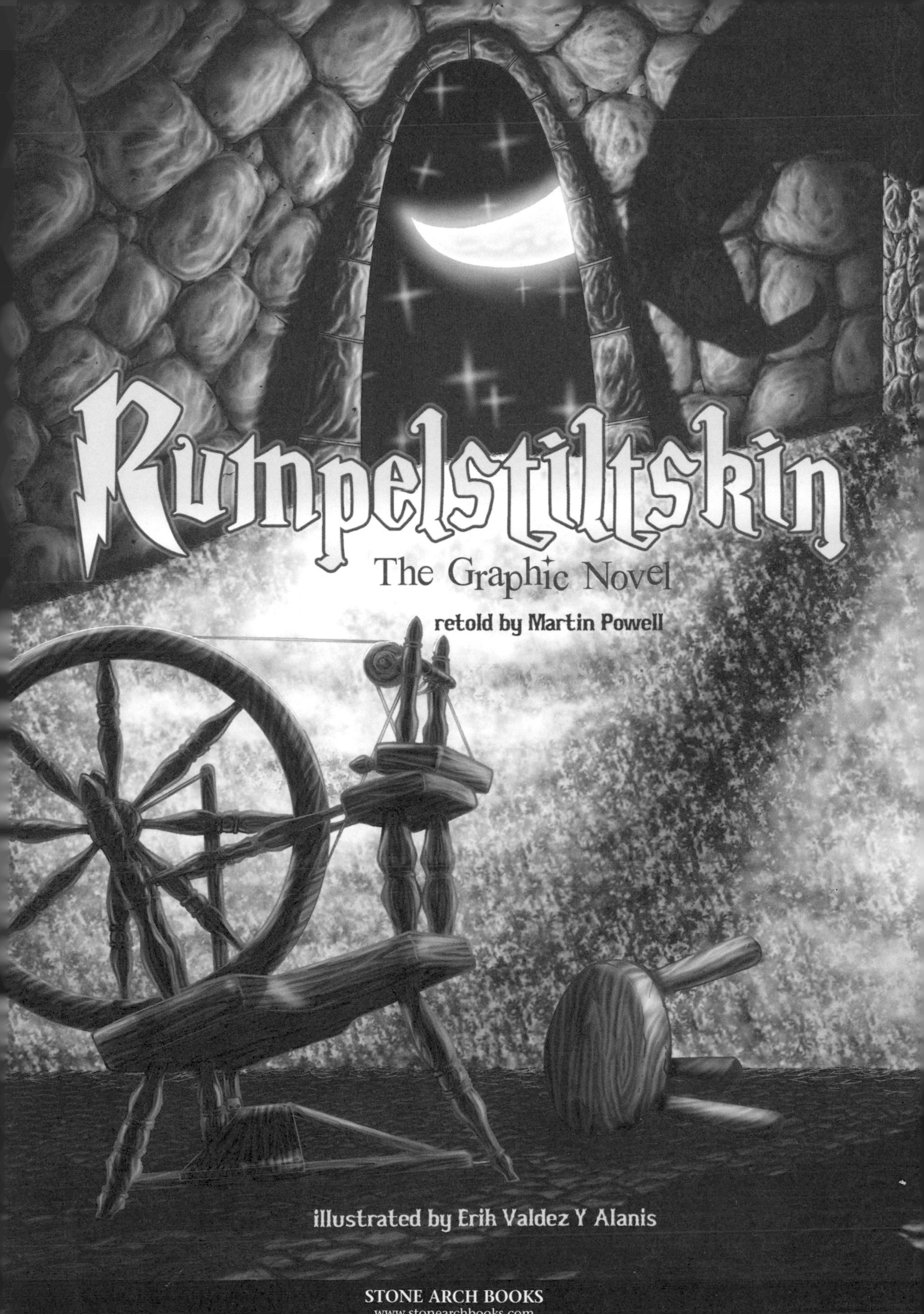

Rumpelstiltskin

The Graphic Novel

retold by Martin Powell

illustrated by Erik Valdez Y Alanis

STONE ARCH BOOKS
www.stonearchbooks.com

Graphic Spin is published by Stone Arch Books
151 Good Counsel Drive, P.O. Box 669
Mankato, Minnesota 56002
www.stonearchbooks.com

Library of Congress Cataloging-in-Publication Data
Powell, Martin.
    Rumpelstiltskin: The Graphic Novel / retold by Martin Powell; illustrated by Erik Valdez Y
Alanis.
    p. cm. — (Graphic Spin)
    ISBN 978-1-4342-0768-5 (library binding)
    ISBN 978-1-4342-0864-4 (pbk.)
    1. Graphic novels. [1. Graphic novels. 2. Fairy tales. 3. Folklore—Germany.] I. Valdez Y Alanis,
Erik, ill. II. Rumpelstiltskin (Folk tale) English. III. Title.
PZ7.7.P69Ru 2009
398.2—dc22   2008006724

Summary: To repay her father's debts, Mirabelle promises the King that she'll spin his straw into
gold. An evil troll agrees to help her for a price. Now, Mirabelle must repay an even greater debt,
unless she can guess the terrible creature's name.

Art Director: Heather Kindseth
Graphic Designer: Kay Fraser

Librarian Reviewer
Katharine Kan
Graphic novel reviewer and Library Consultant, Panama City, FL
MLS in Library and Information Studies, University of Hawaii at Manoa, HI

Reading Consultant
Elizabeth Stedem
Educator/Consultant, Colorado Springs, CO
MA in Elementary Education, University of Denver, CO

1 2 3 4 5 6 13 12 11 10 09 08

Printed in the United States of America

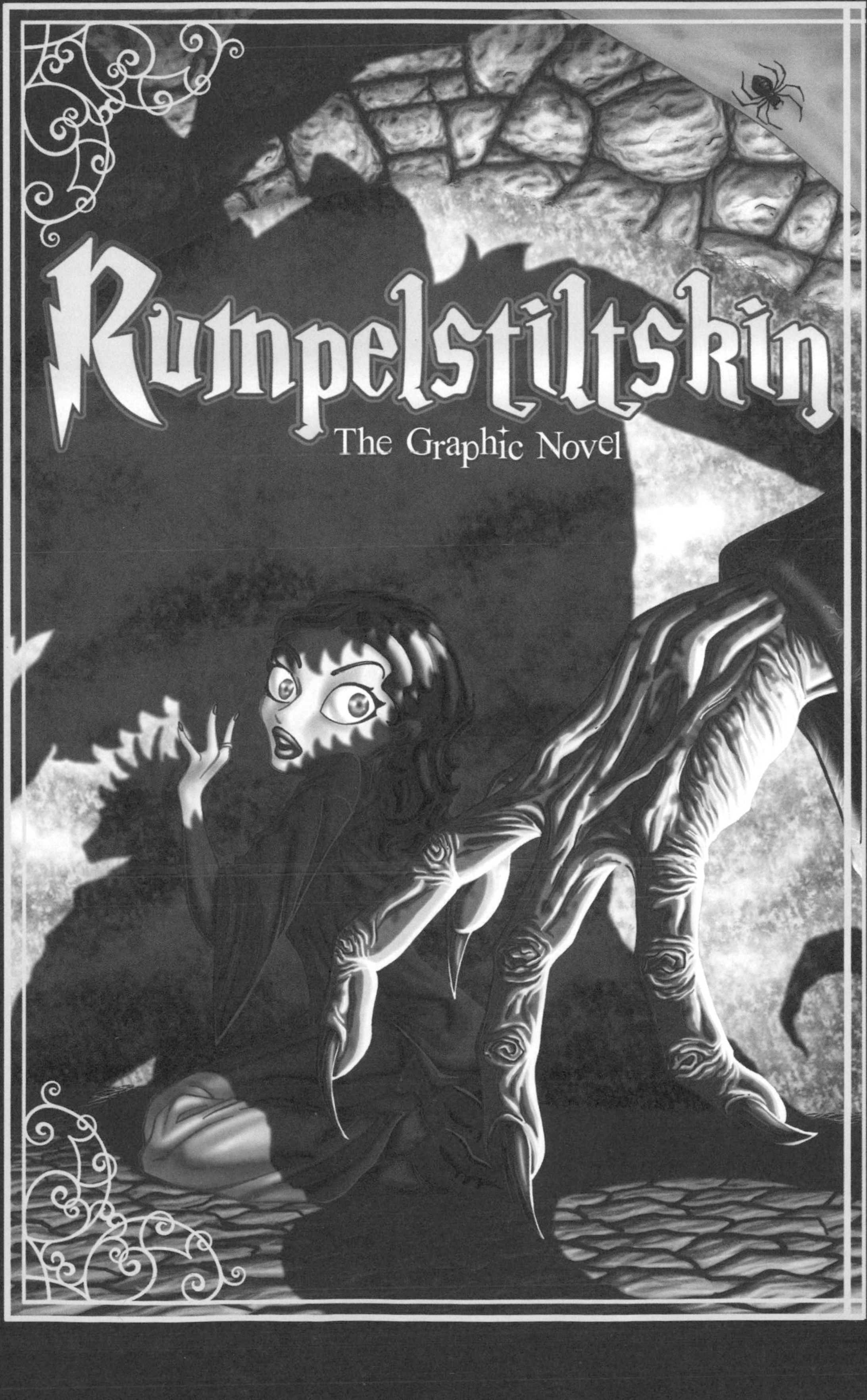
Rumpelstiltskin
The Graphic Novel

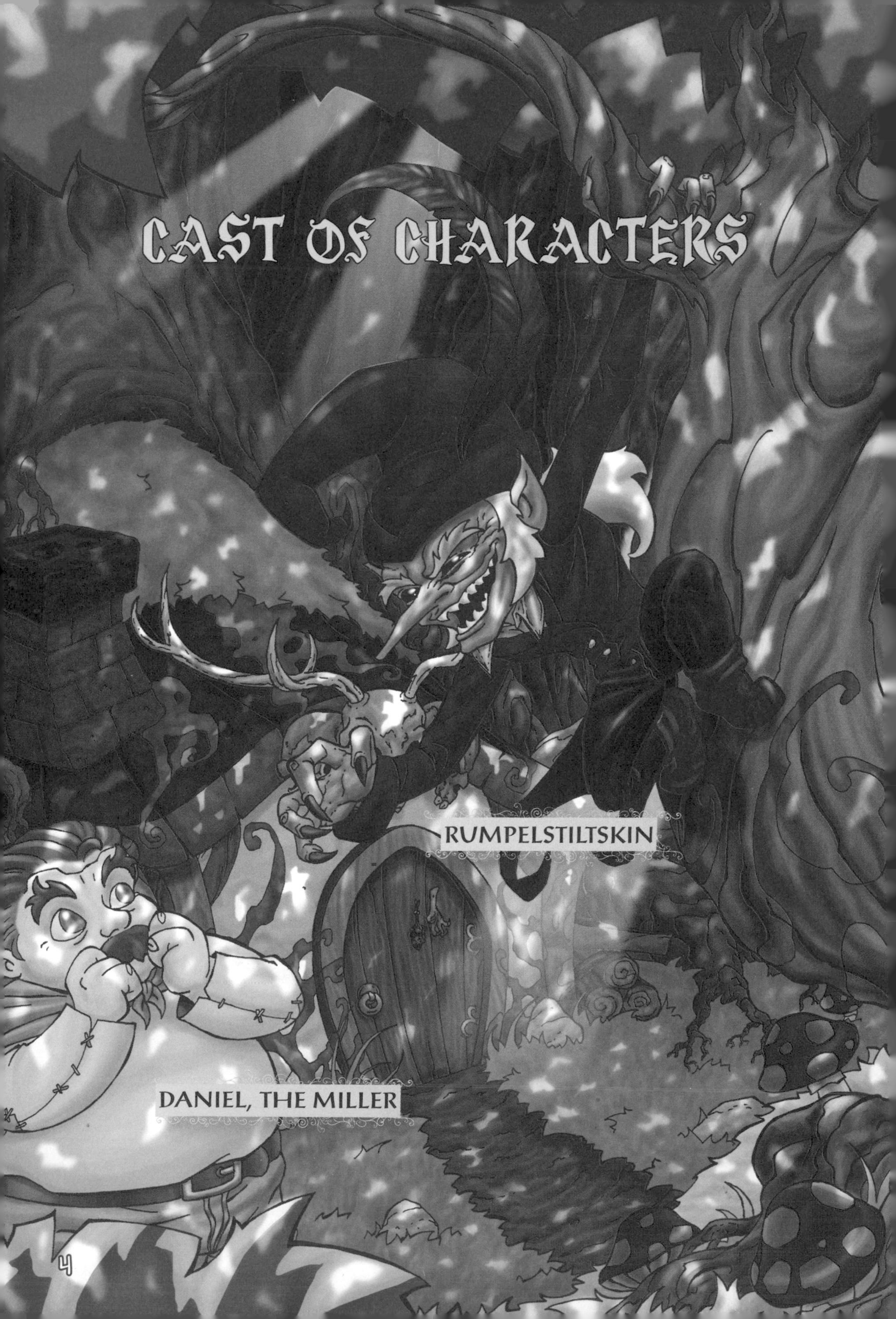
CAST OF CHARACTERS
RUMPELSTILTSKIN
DANIEL, THE MILLER

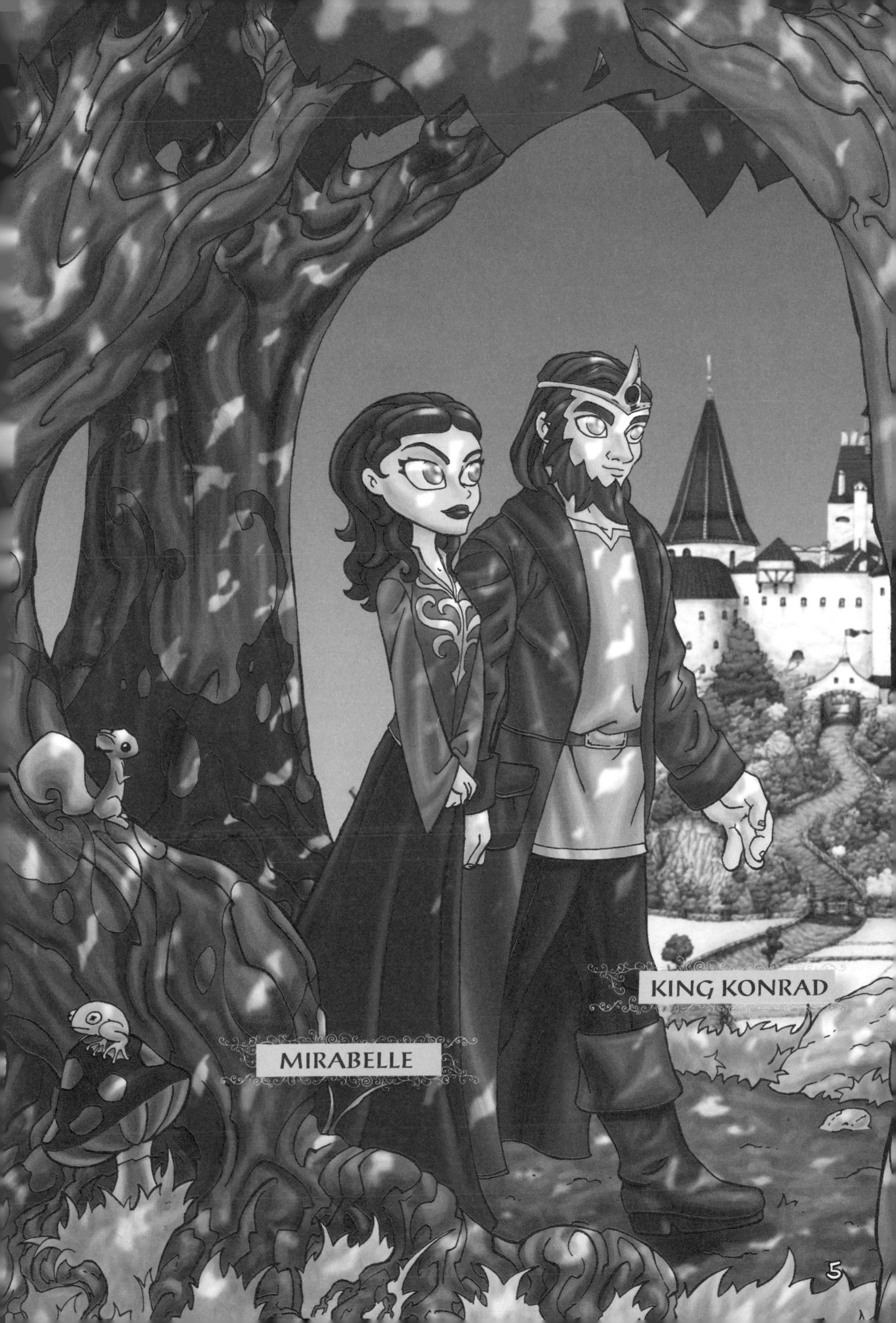
KING KONRAD
MIRABELLE

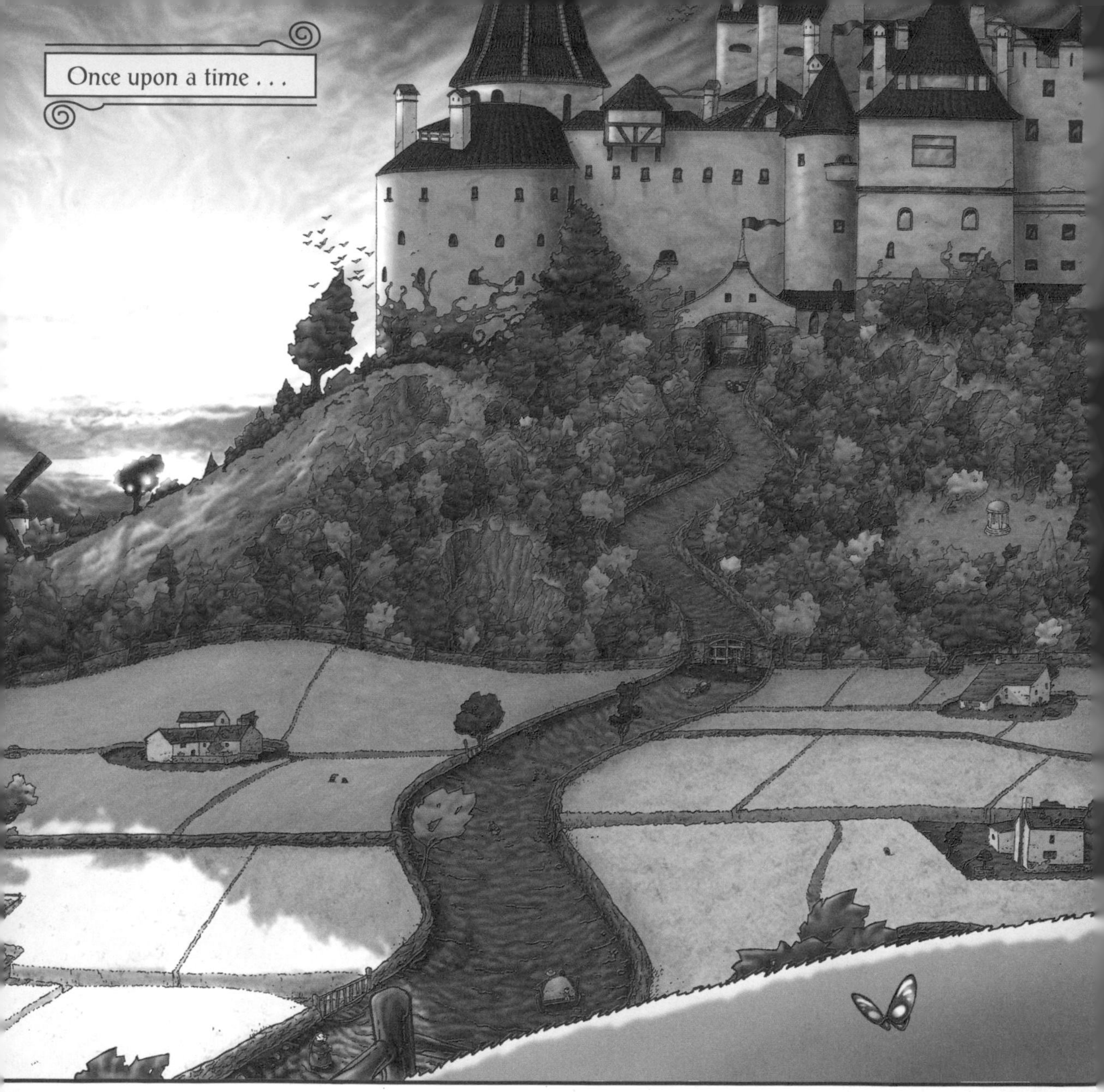
Once upon a time . . .

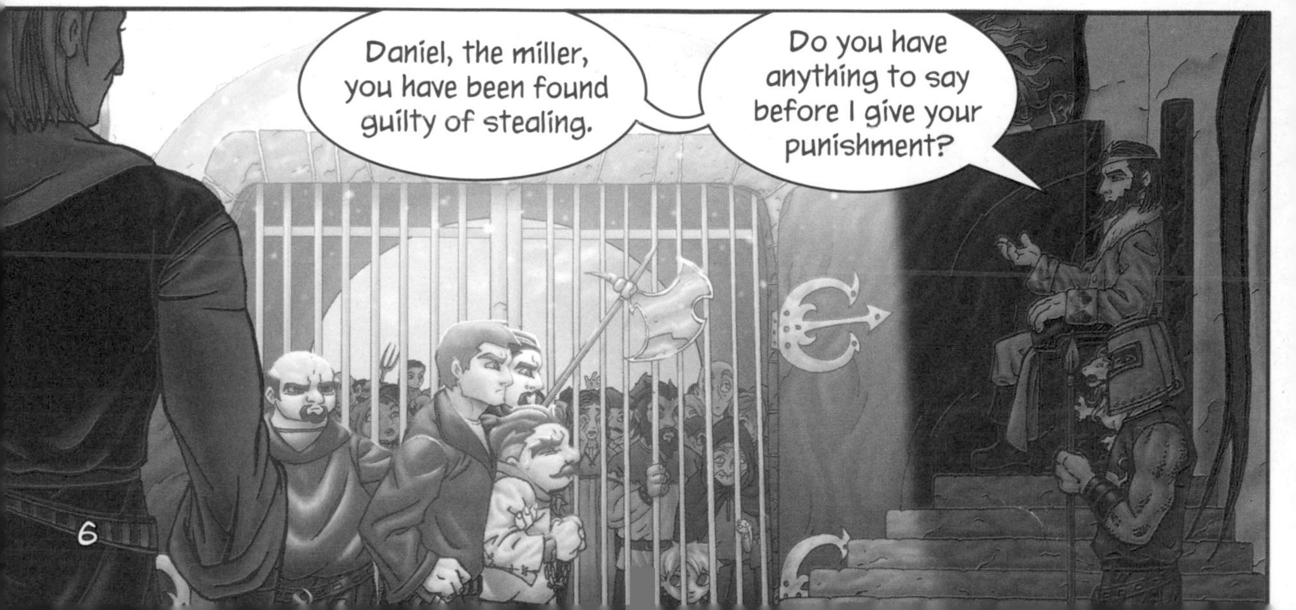
Daniel, the miller, you have been found guilty of stealing.
Do you have anything to say before I give your punishment?

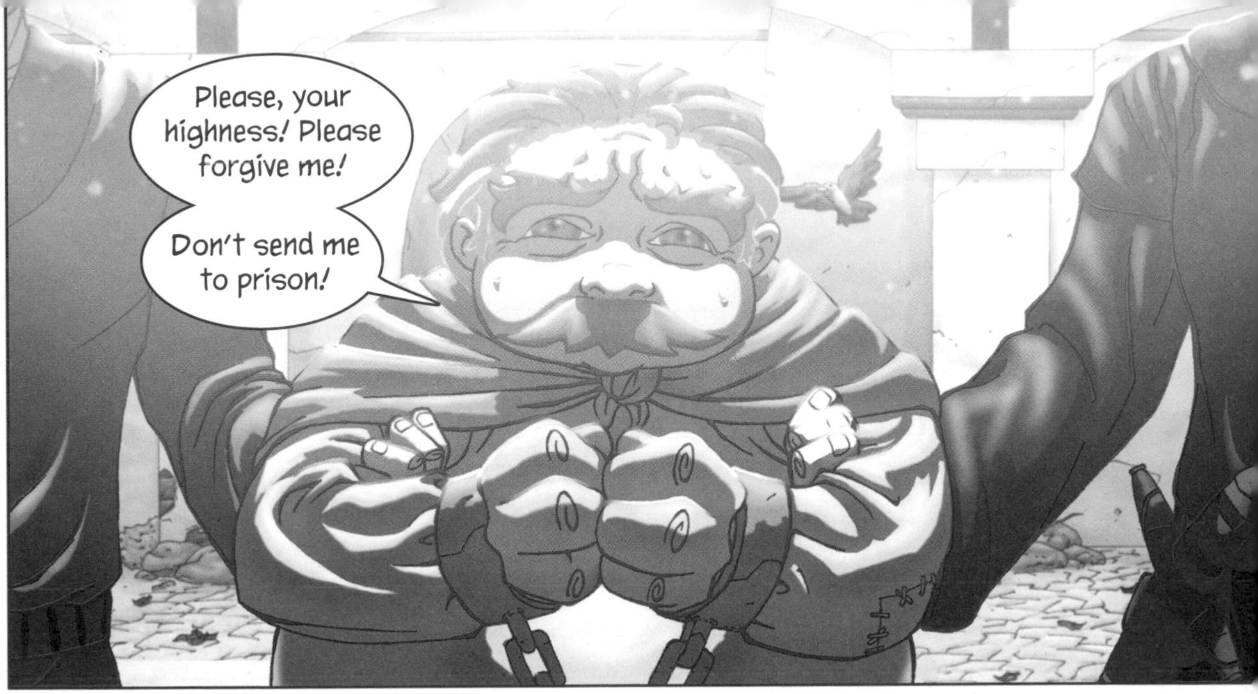
Please, your highness! Please forgive me!
Don't send me to prison!

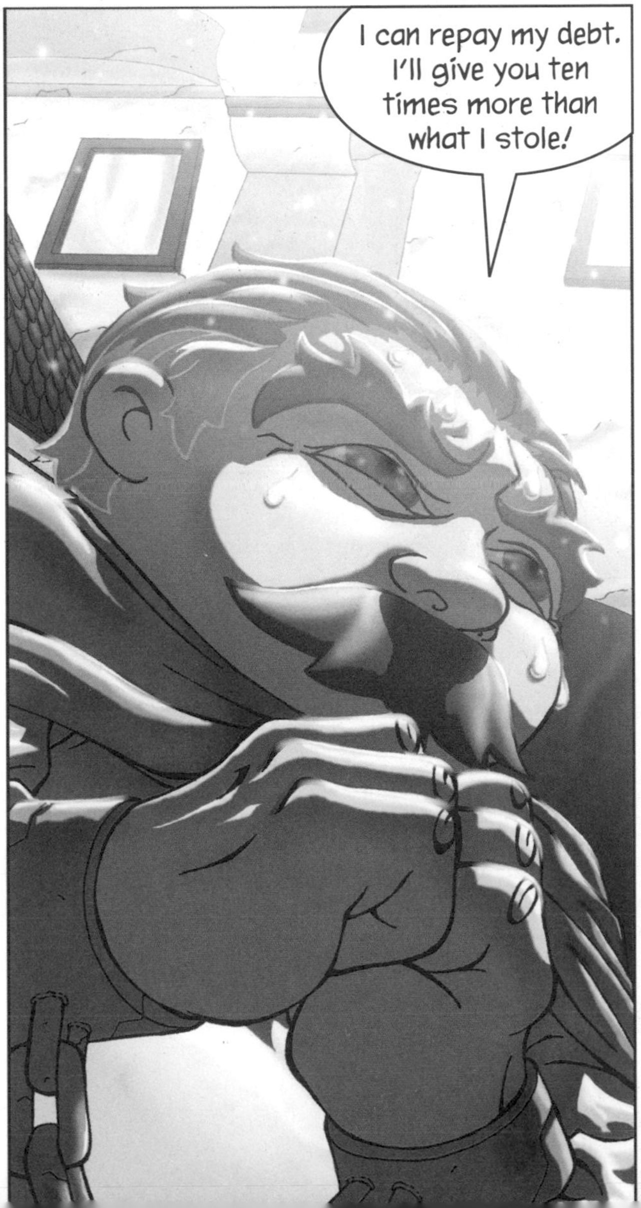
I can repay my debt. I'll give you ten times more than what I stole!

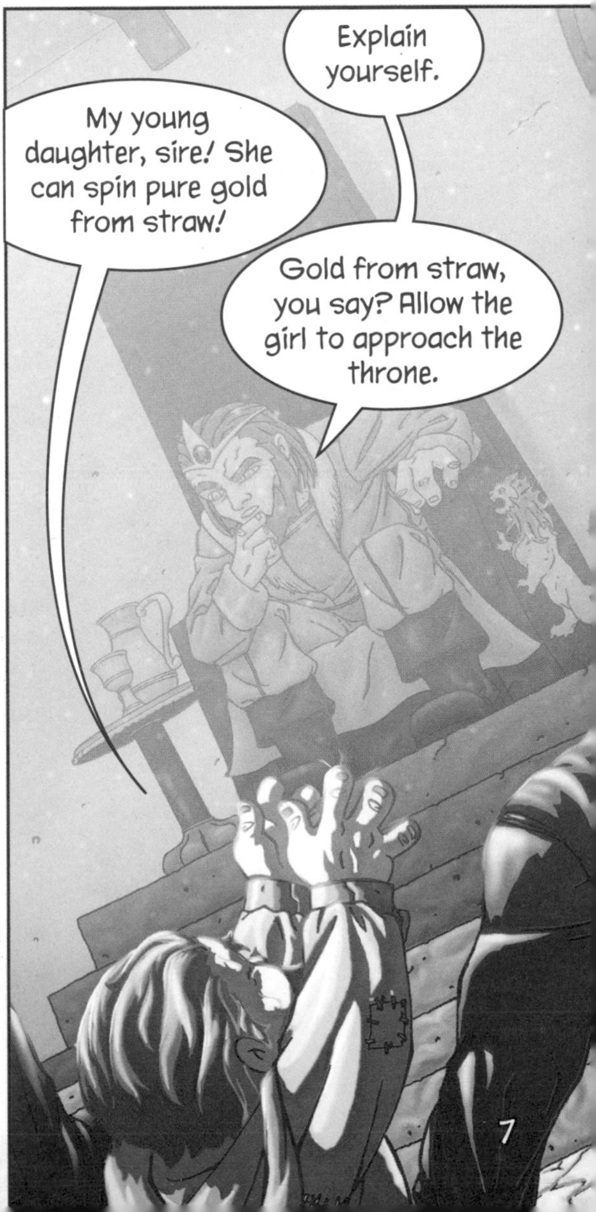
Explain yourself.
My young daughter, sire! She can spin pure gold from straw!
Gold from straw, you say? Allow the girl to approach the throne.

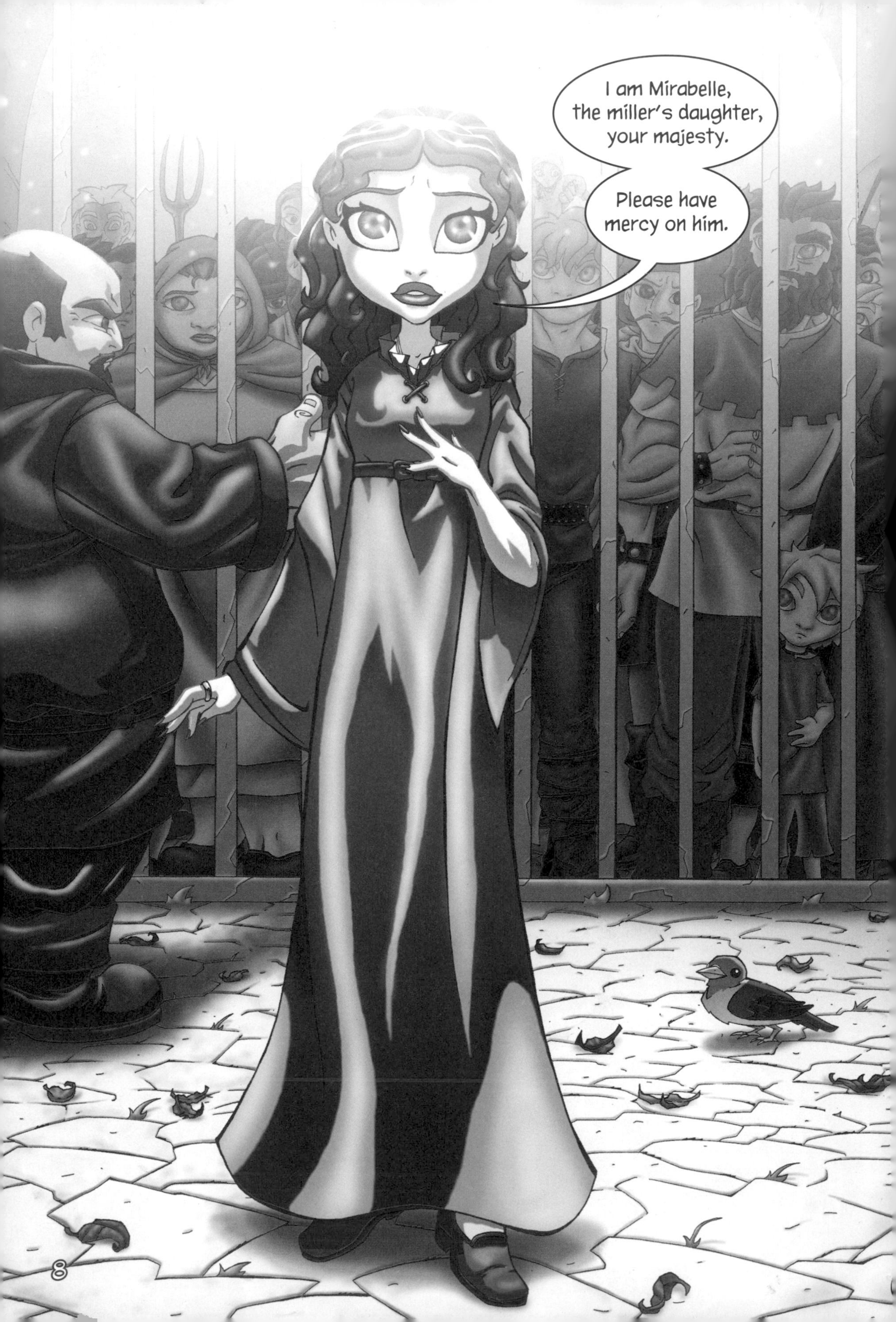
I am Mirabelle, the miller's daughter, your majesty.
Please have mercy on him.

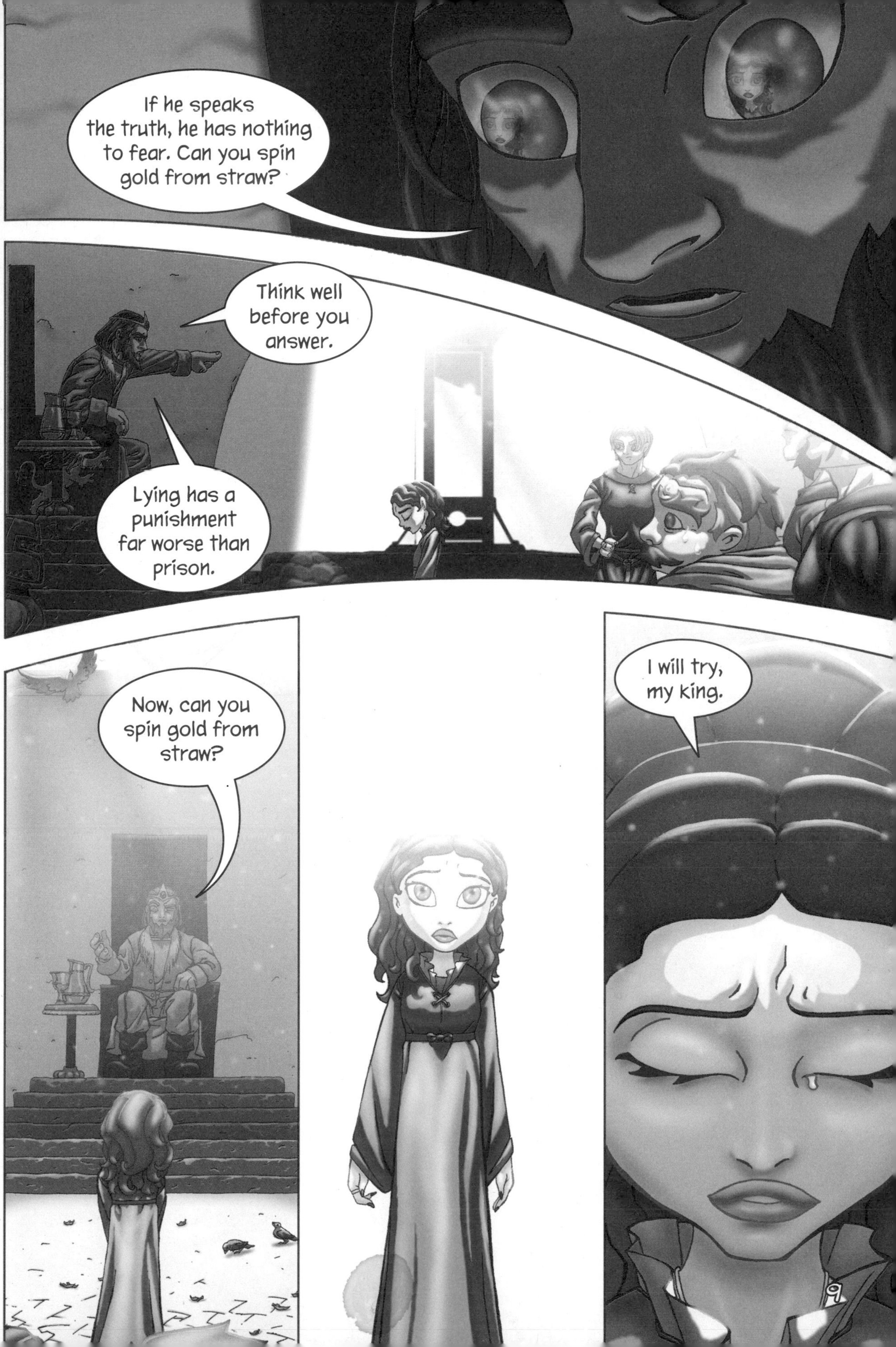
If he speaks the truth, he has nothing to fear. Can you spin gold from straw?
Think well before you answer.
Lying has a punishment far worse than prison.
Now, can you spin gold from straw?
I will try, my king.

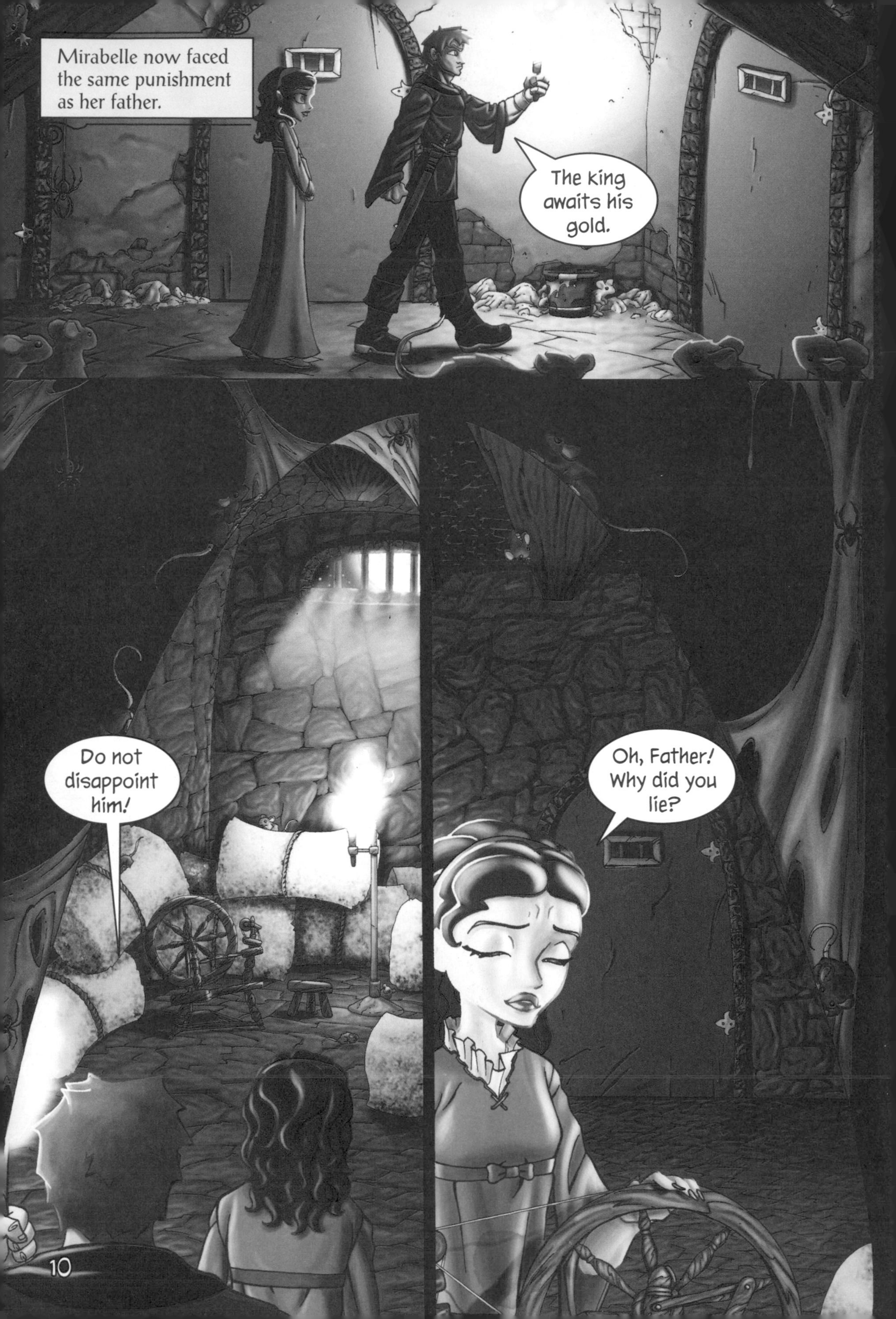
Mirabelle now faced the same punishment as her father.
The king awaits his gold.
Do not disappoint him!
Oh, Father! Why did you lie?

Turning straw into gold is impossible!
It's hopeless.
Looks like you could use a friend.
Ahh!

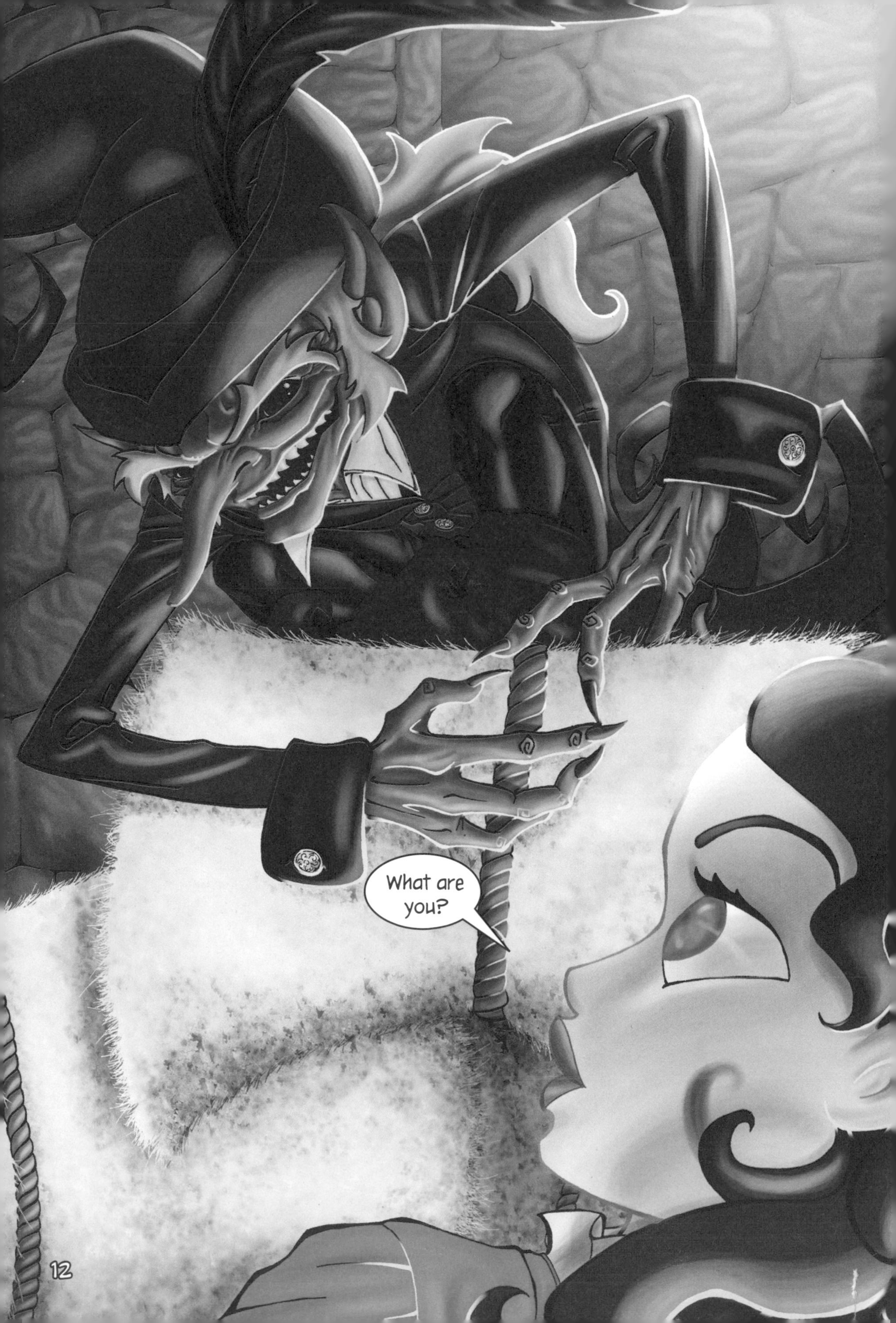
What are you?

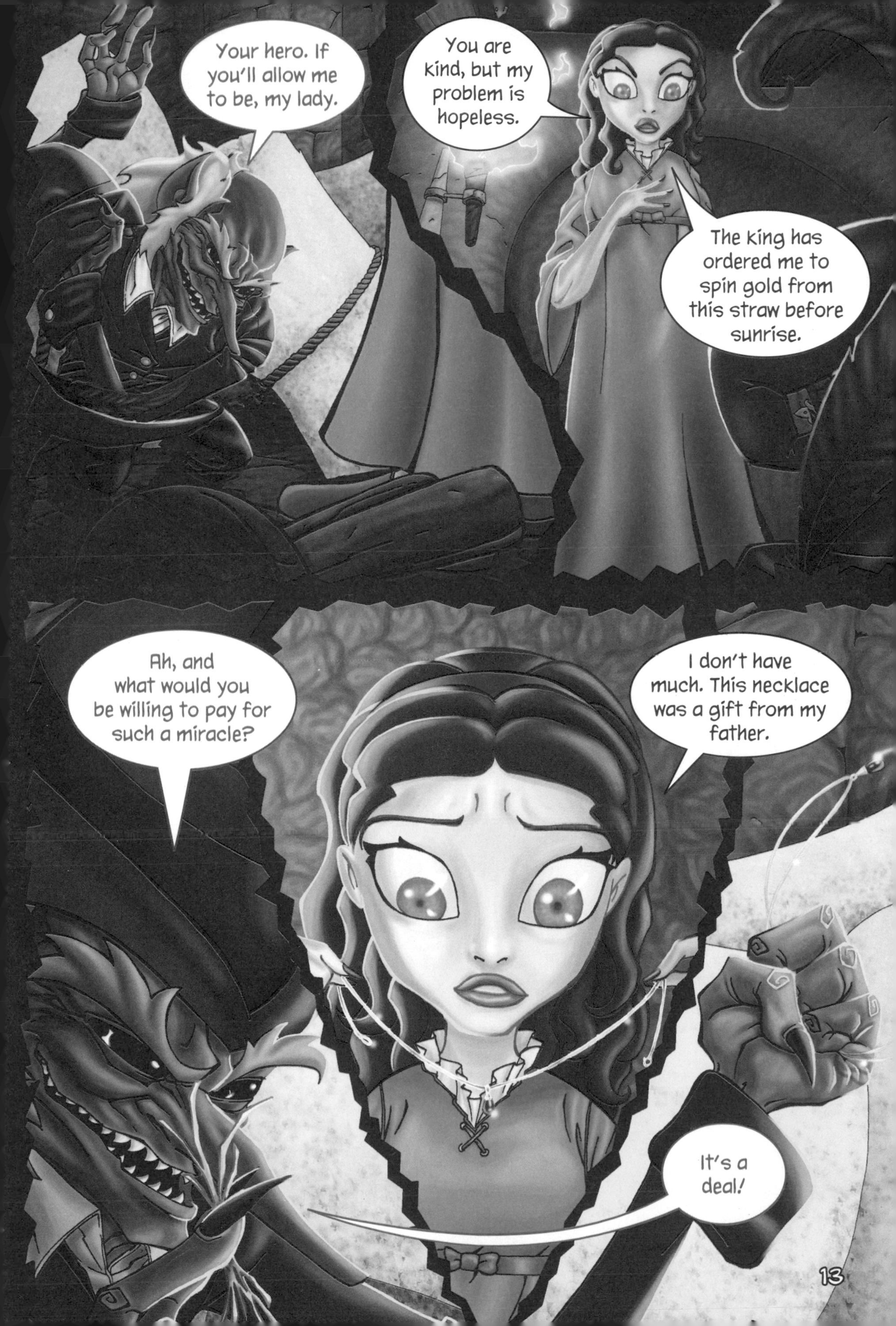
Your hero. If you'll allow me to be, my lady.
You are kind, but my problem is hopeless.
The king has ordered me to spin gold from this straw before sunrise.
Ah, and what would you be willing to pay for such a miracle?
I don't have much. This necklace was a gift from my father.
It's a deal!

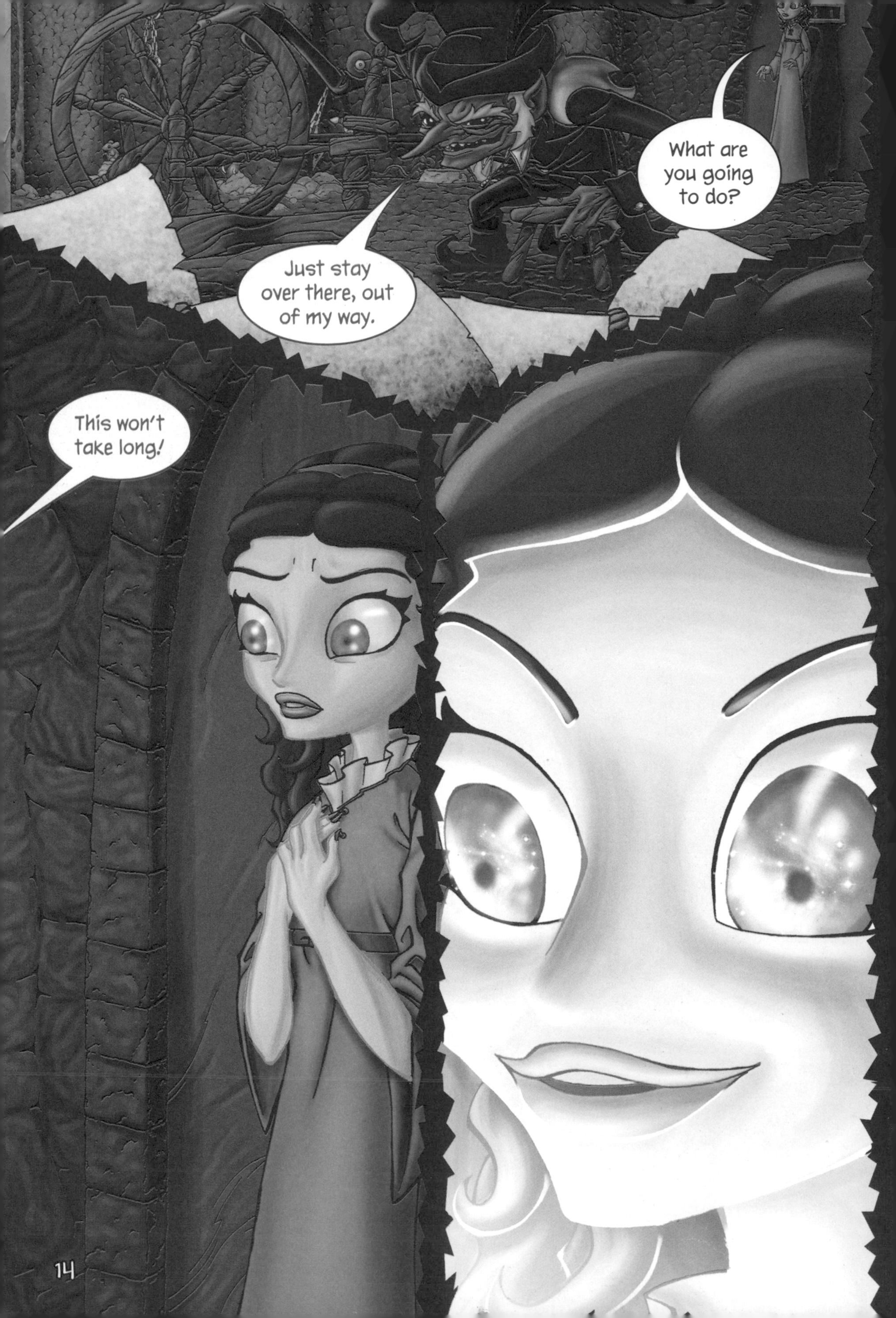
What are you going to do?
Just stay over there, out of my way.
This won't take long!

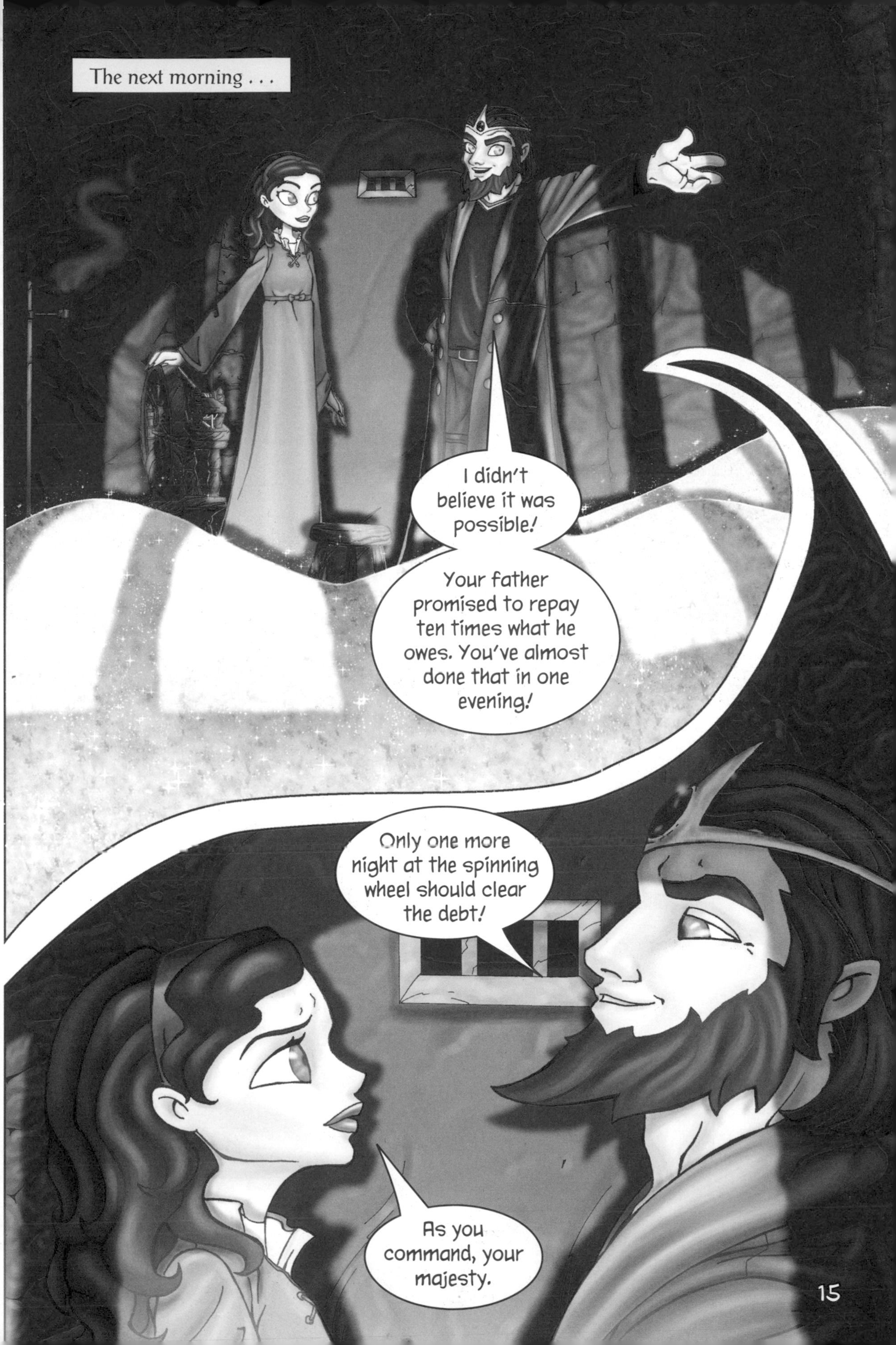
The next morning . . .
I didn't believe it was possible!
Your father promised to repay ten times what he owes. You've almost done that in one evening!
Only one more night at the spinning wheel should clear the debt!
As you command, your majesty.

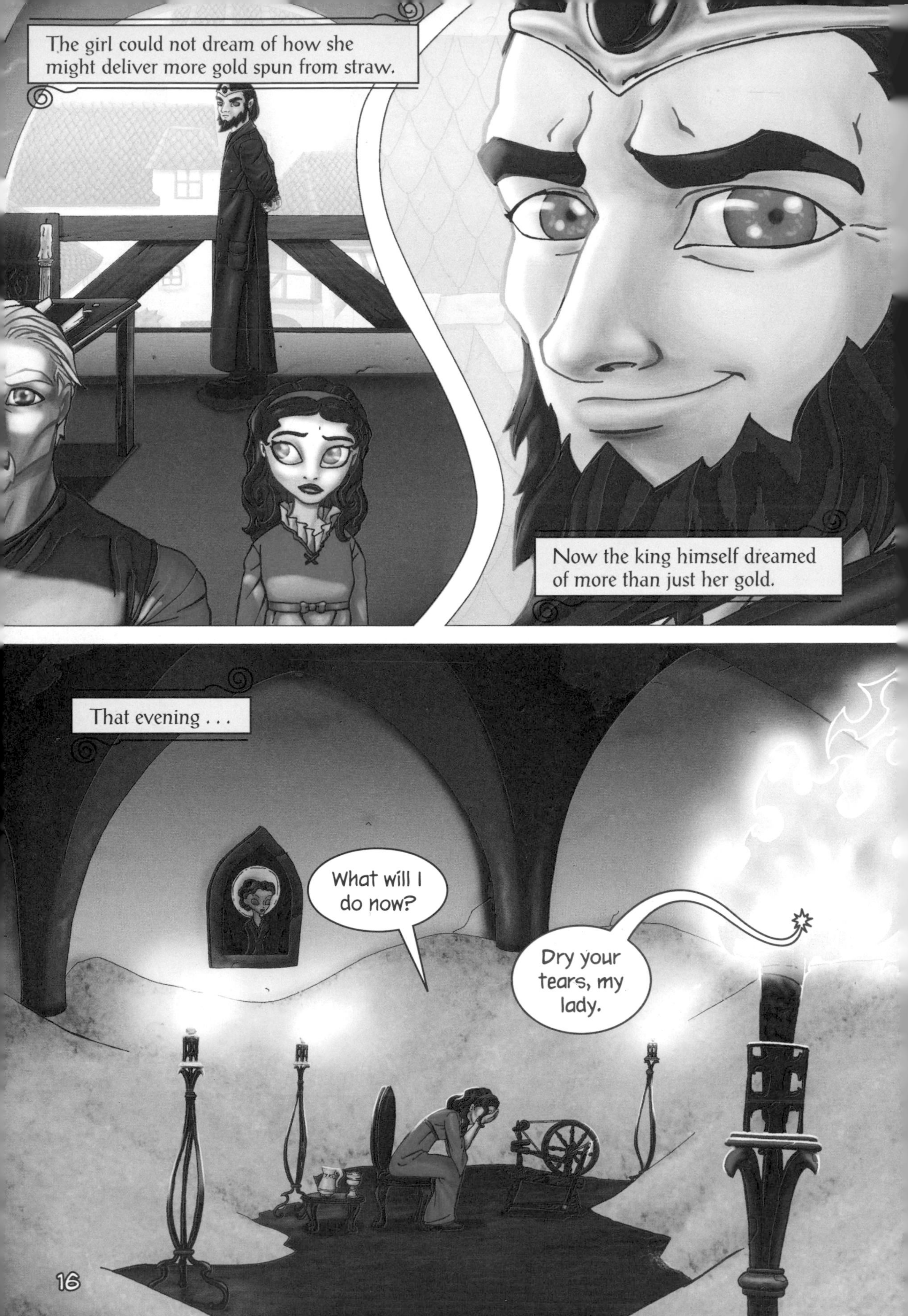

The girl could not dream of how she might deliver more gold spun from straw.
Now the king himself dreamed of more than just her gold.
That evening . . .
What will I do now?
Dry your tears, my lady.

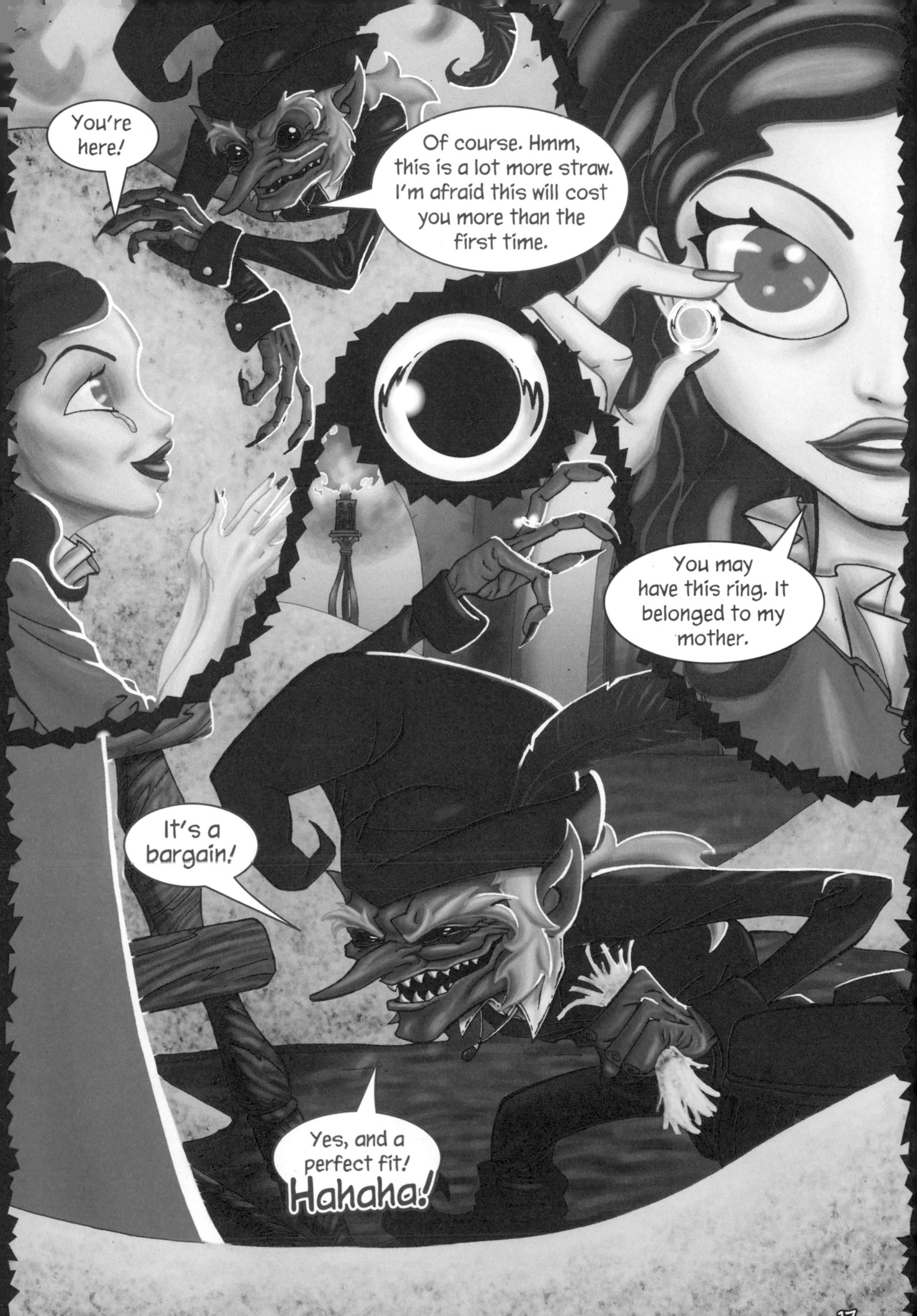
You're here!
Of course. Hmm, this is a lot more straw. I'm afraid this will cost you more than the first time.
You may have this ring. It belonged to my mother.
It's a bargain!
Yes, and a perfect fit! Hahaha!

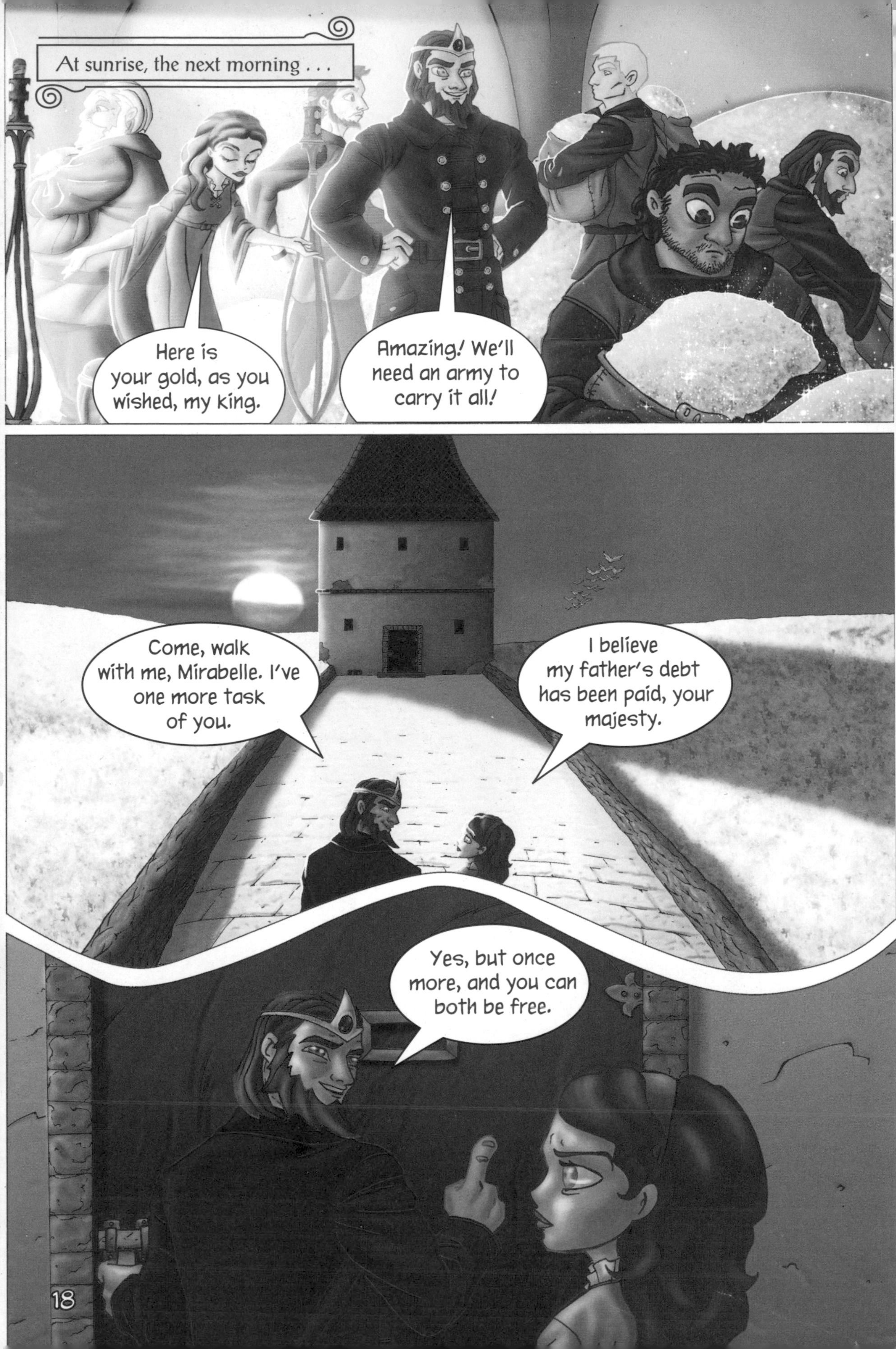
At sunrise, the next morning . . .
Here is your gold, as you wished, my king.
Amazing! We'll need an army to carry it all!
Come, walk with me, Mirabelle. I've one more task of you.
I believe my father's debt has been paid, your majesty.
Yes, but once more, and you can both be free.

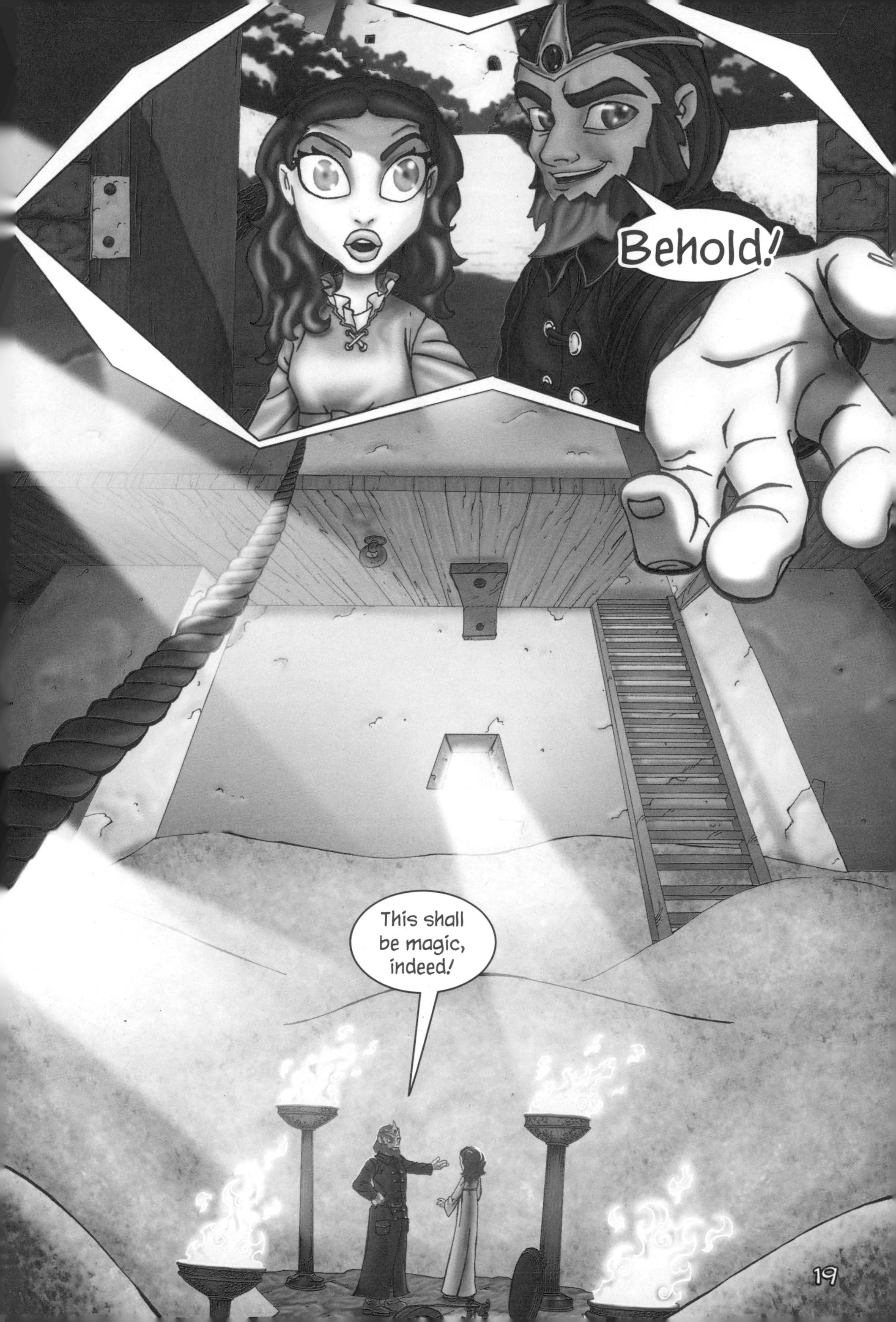
Behold!
This shall be magic, indeed!

Later that night, Mirabelle is not alone for long.
You have my necklace and my ring. I have nothing else to give you.
Now, I wouldn't say that. Someday you might be rich.
You might even be queen!
Yes, of course, but—
If such a day ever comes, say a year from now, would you be willing to pay my price?
Done!

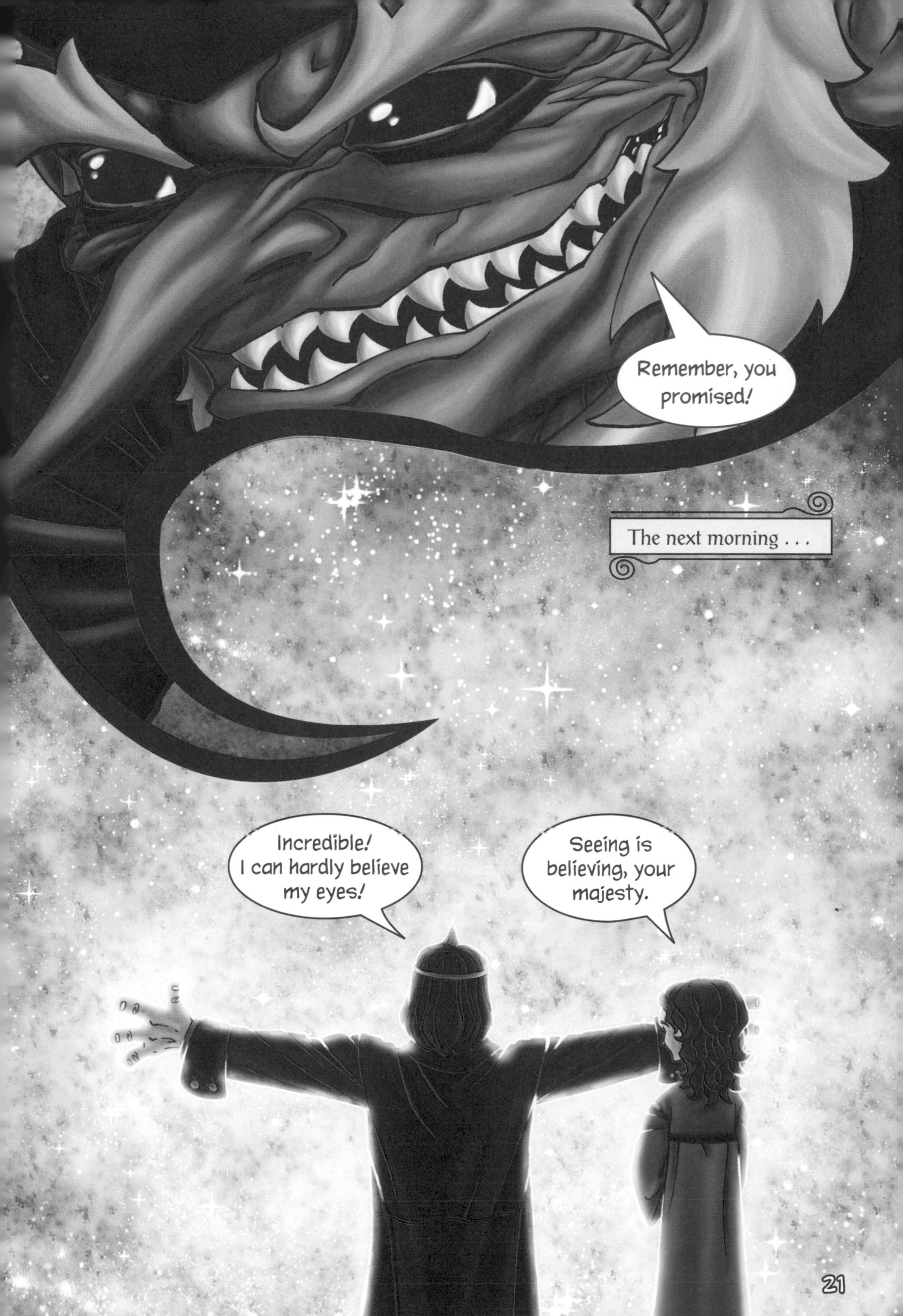
Remember, you promised!
The next morning . . .
Incredible! I can hardly believe my eyes!
Seeing is believing, your majesty.

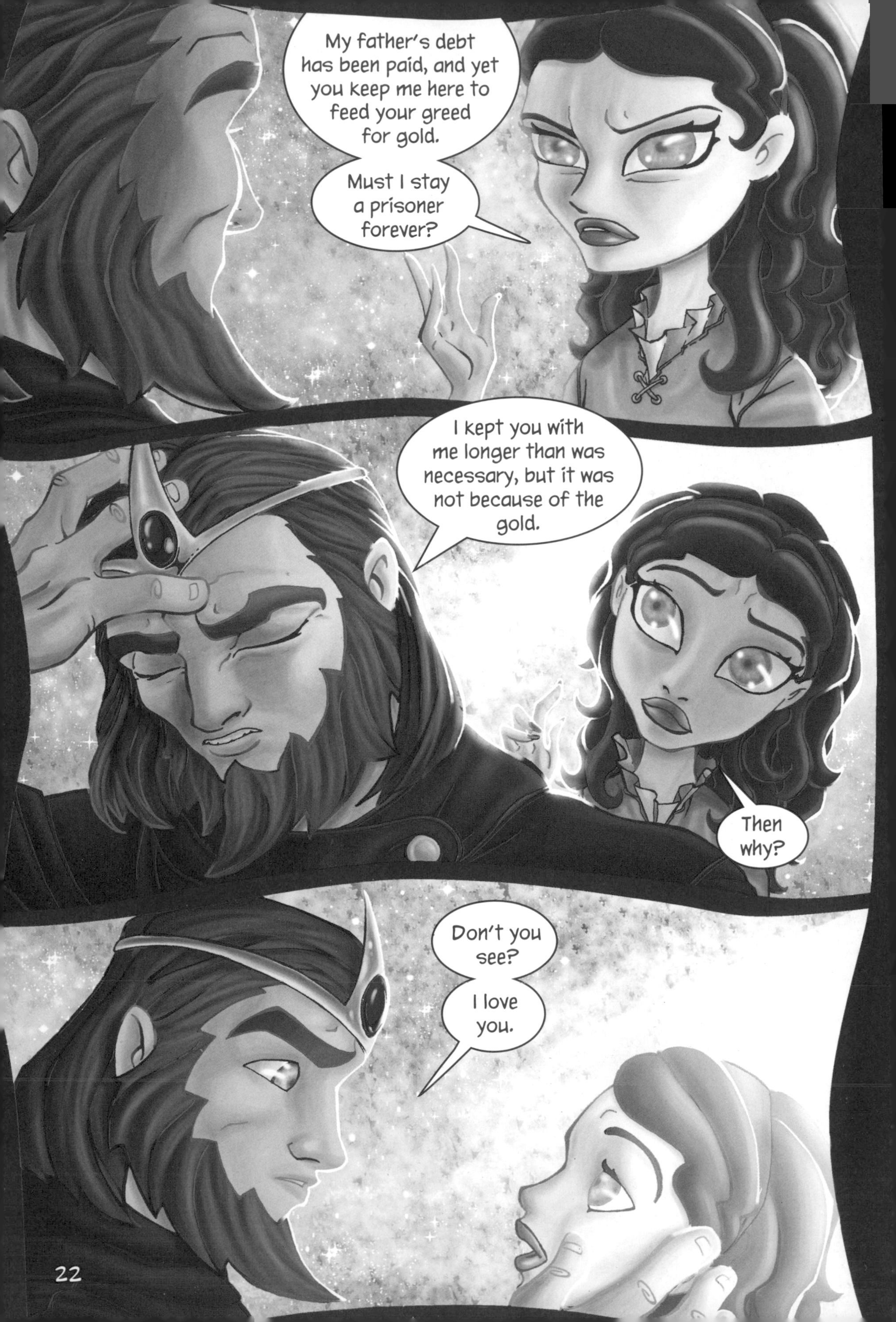
My father's debt has been paid, and yet you keep me here to feed your greed for gold.
Must I stay a prisoner forever?
I kept you with me longer than was necessary, but it was not because of the gold.
Then why?
Don't you see?
I love you.

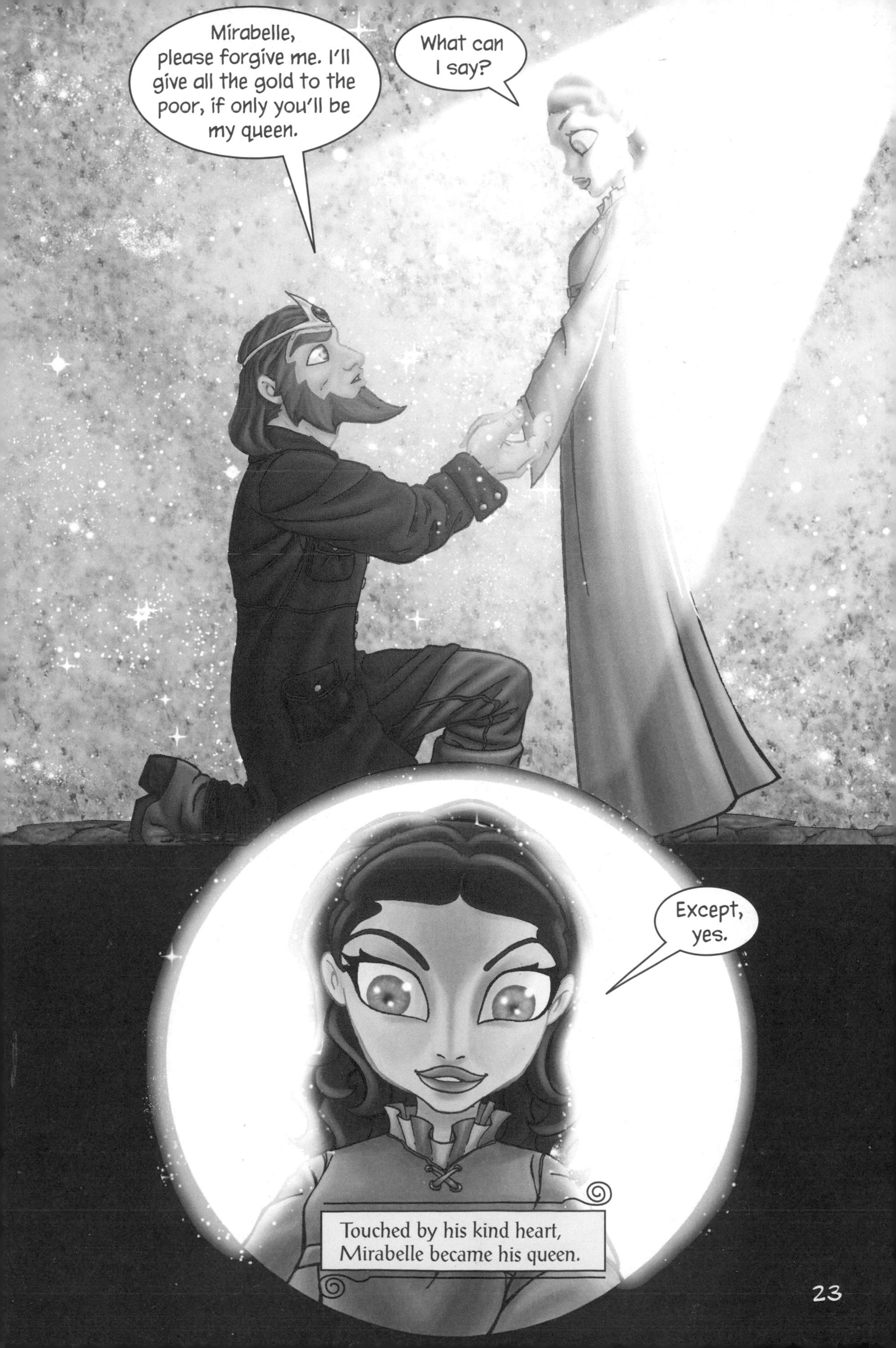
Mirabelle, please forgive me. I'll give all the gold to the poor, if only you'll be my queen.
What can I say?
Except, yes.
Touched by his kind heart, Mirabelle became his queen.

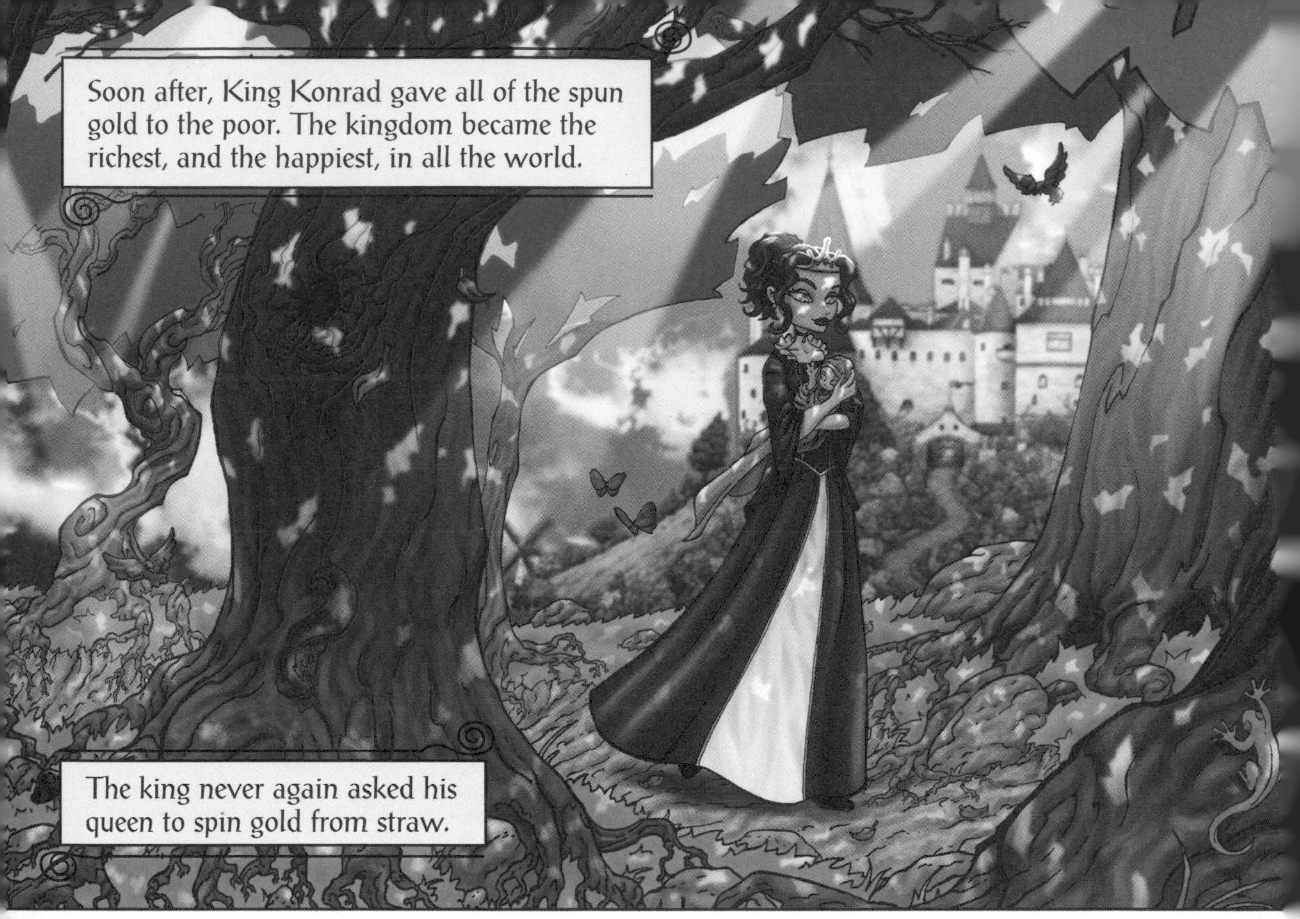
Soon after, King Konrad gave all of the spun gold to the poor. The kingdom became the richest, and the happiest, in all the world.
The king never again asked his queen to spin gold from straw.

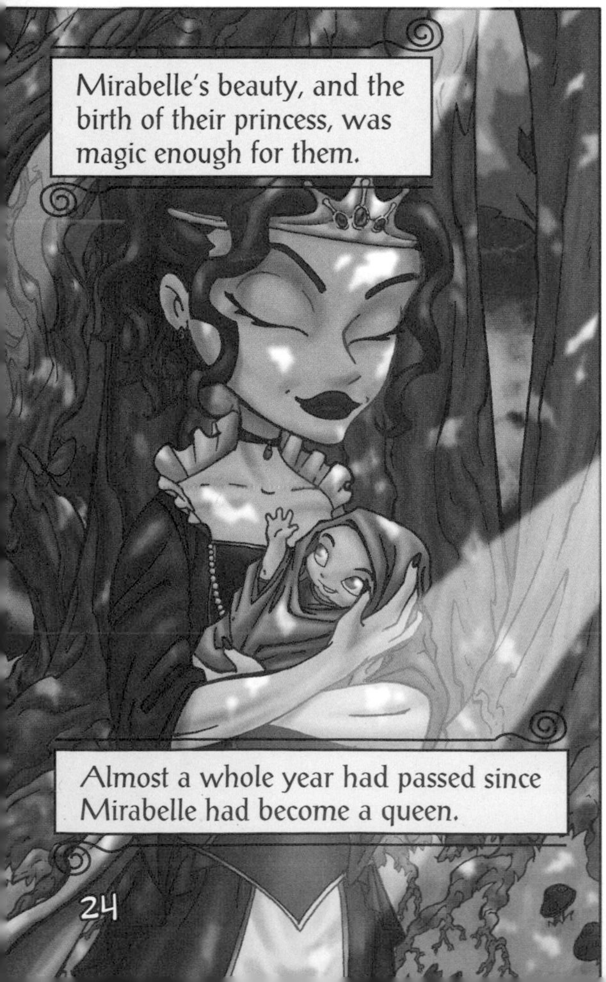
Mirabelle's beauty, and the birth of their princess, was magic enough for them.
Almost a whole year had passed since Mirabelle had become a queen.

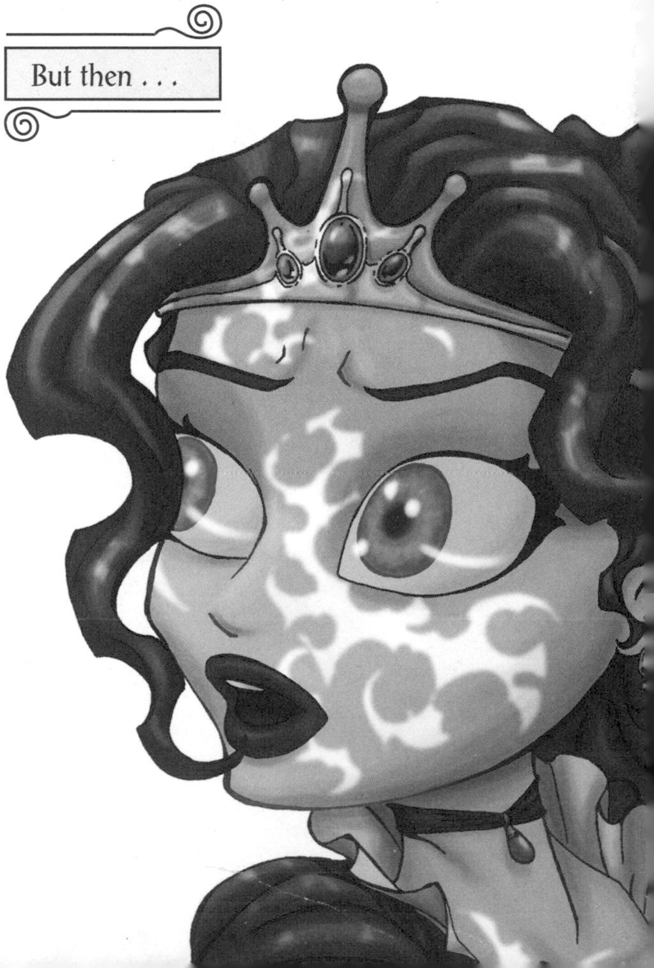
But then . . .

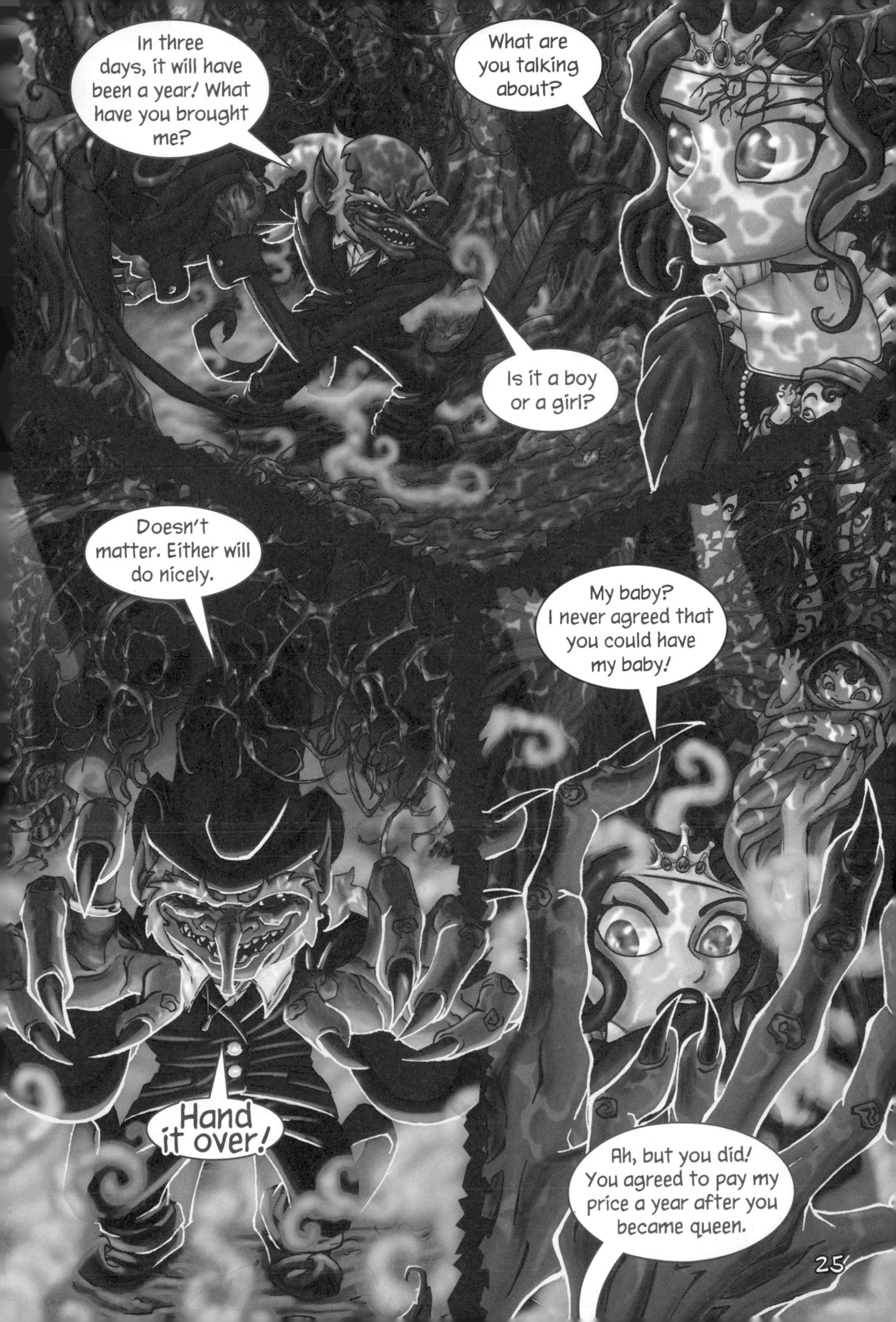
In three days, it will have been a year! What have you brought me?
What are you talking about?
Is it a boy or a girl?
Doesn't matter. Either will do nicely.
My baby? I never agreed that you could have my baby!
Hand it over!
Ah, but you did! You agreed to pay my price a year after you became queen.

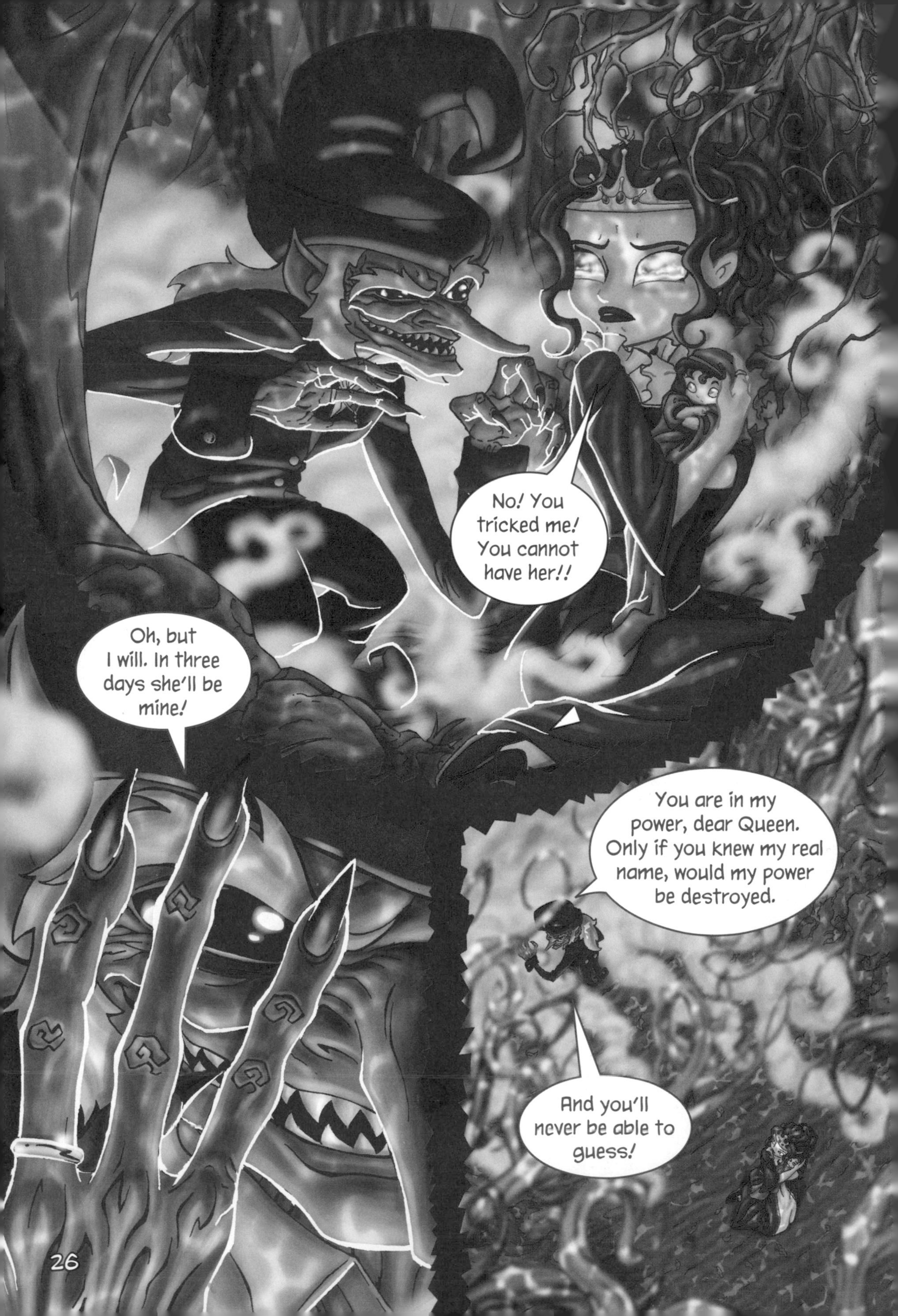
No! You tricked me! You cannot have her!!
Oh, but I will. In three days she'll be mine!
You are in my power, dear Queen. Only if you knew my real name, would my power be destroyed.
And you'll never be able to guess!

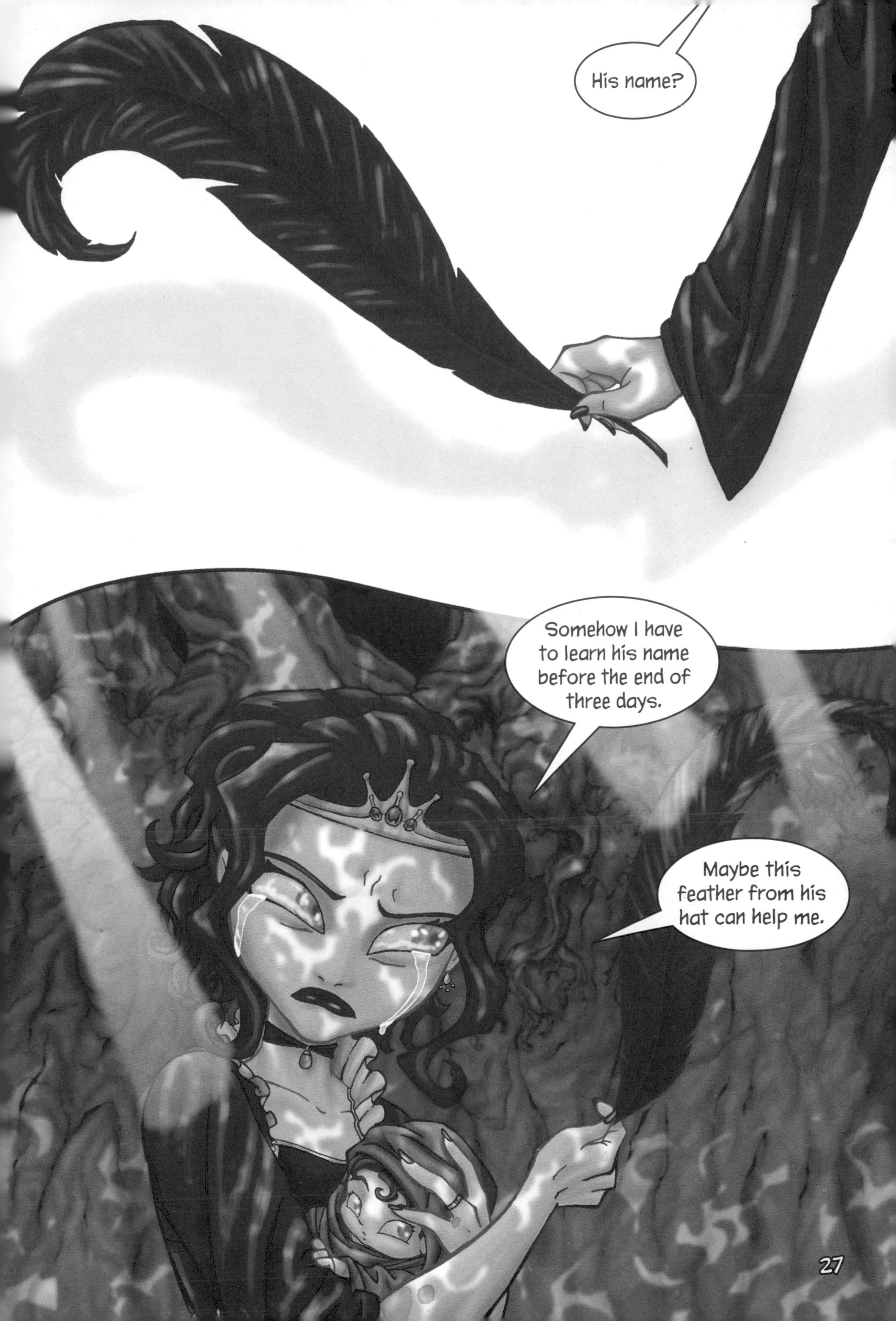
His name?
Somehow I have to learn his name before the end of three days.
Maybe this feather from his hat can help me.

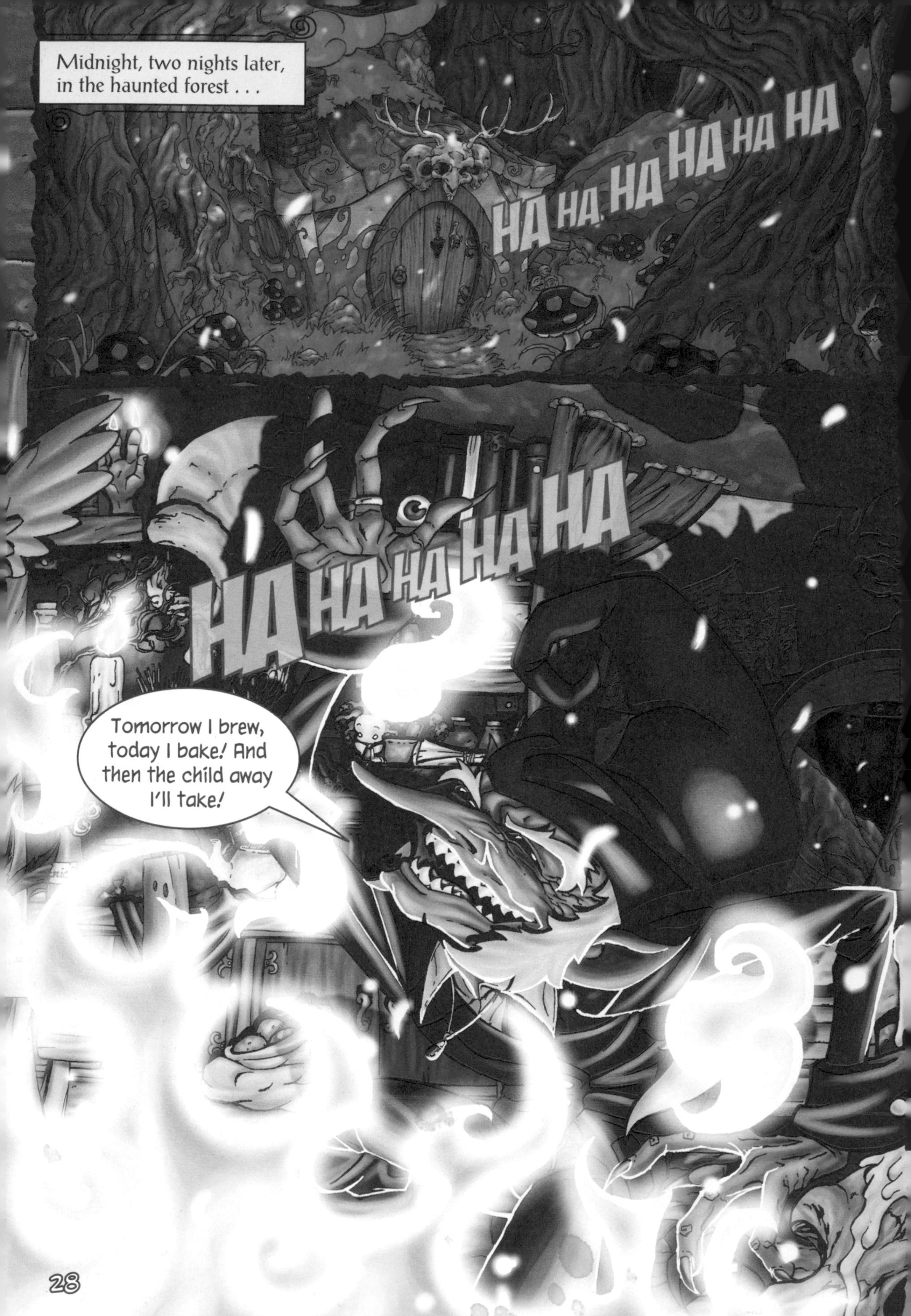
Midnight, two nights later, in the haunted forest . . .
HA HA HA HA HA HA HA
HA HA HA HA HA
Tomorrow I brew, today I bake! And then the child away I'll take!

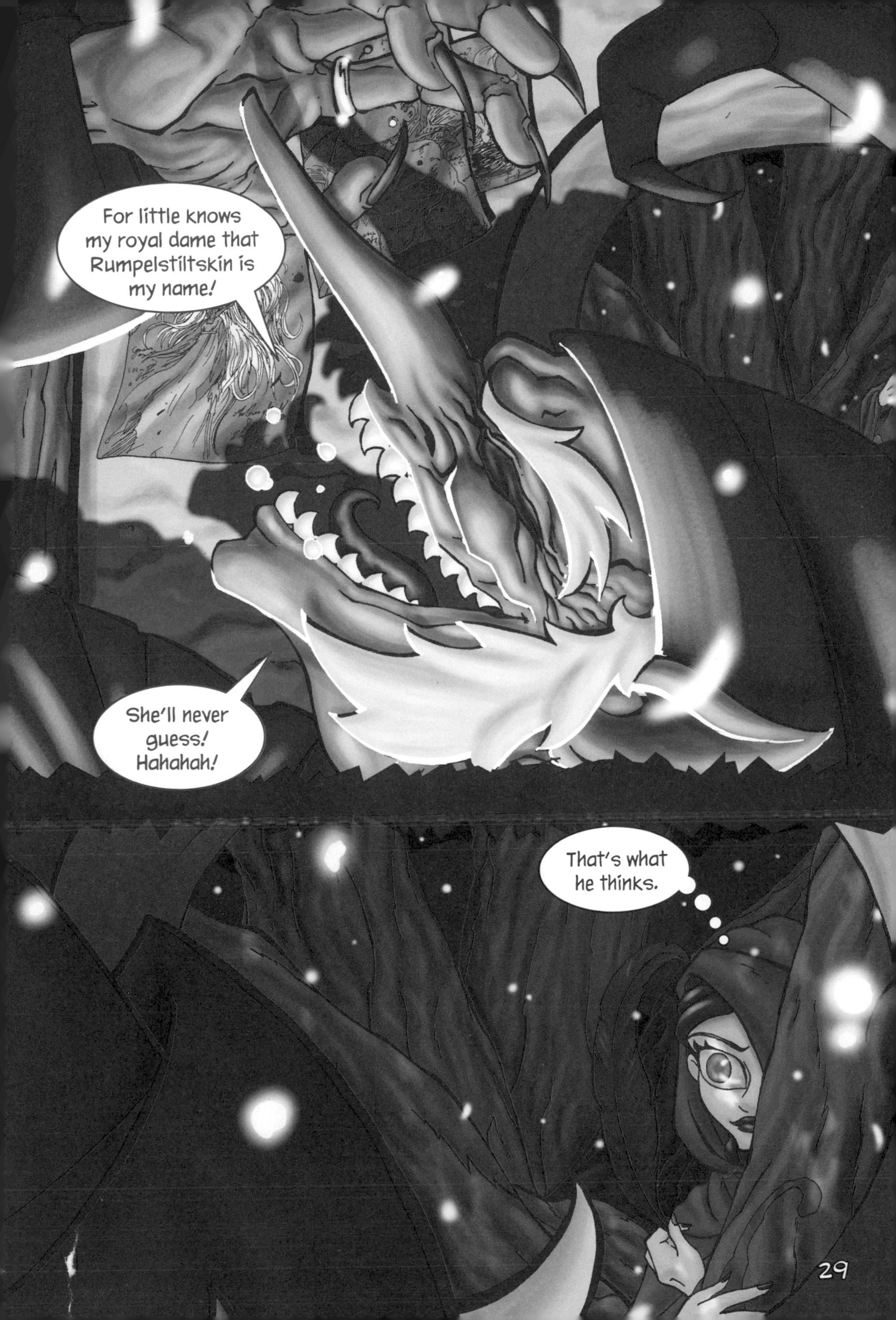
For little knows my royal dame that Rumpelstiltskin is my name!
She'll never guess! Hahahah!
That's what he thinks.

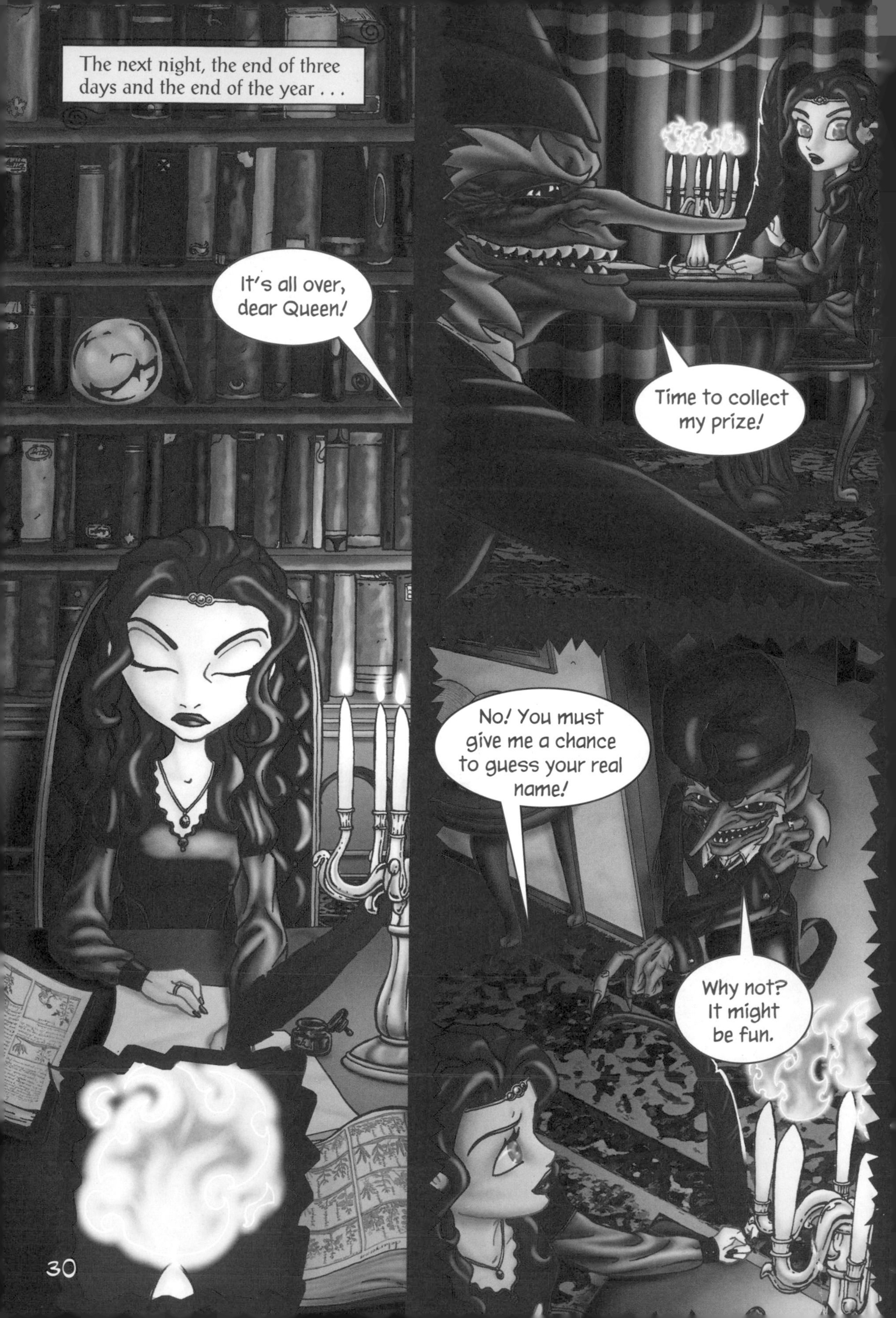
The next night, the end of three days and the end of the year . . .
It's all over, dear Queen!
Time to collect my prize!
No! You must give me a chance to guess your real name!
Why not? It might be fun.

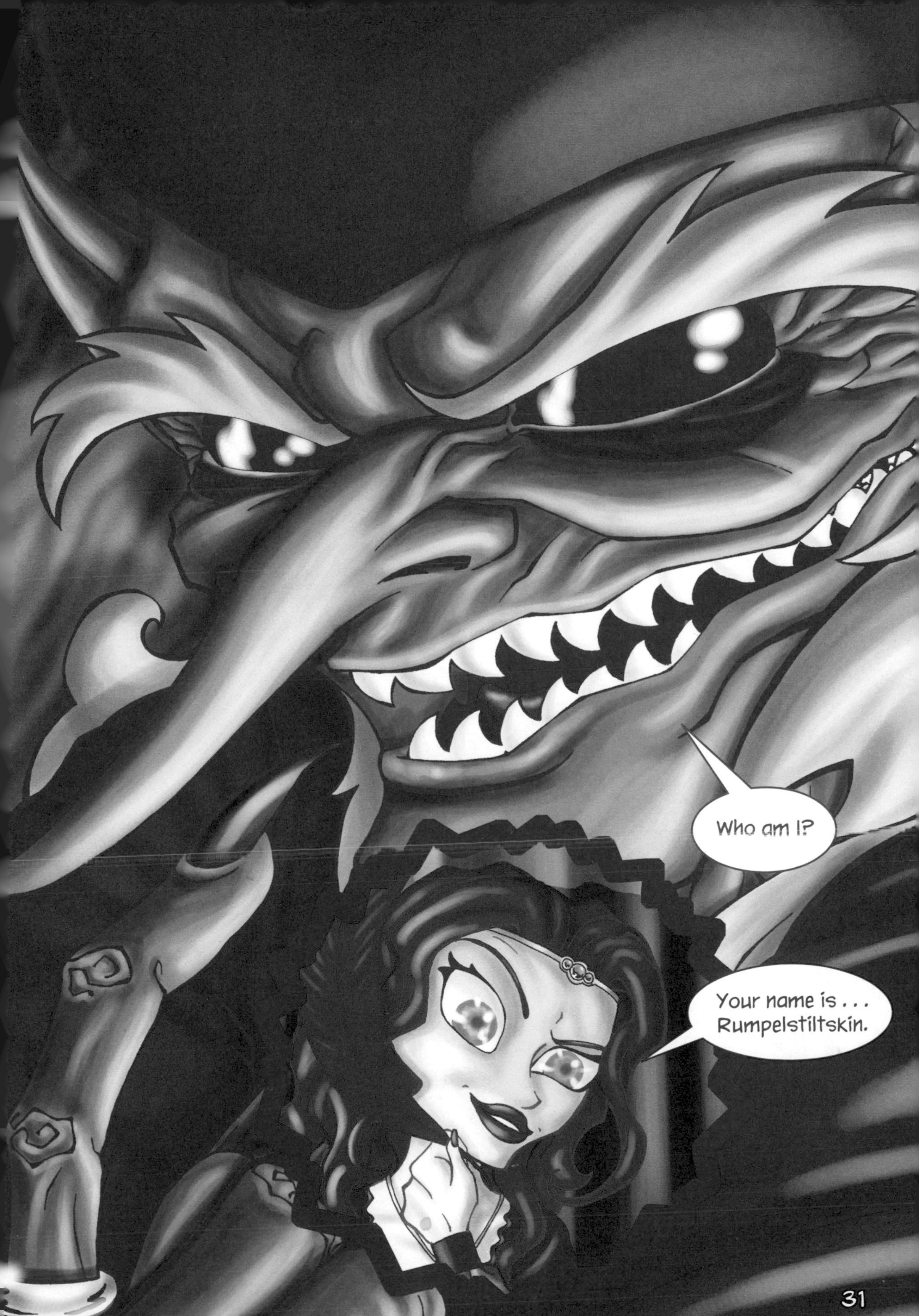
Who am I?
Your name is . . . Rumpelstiltskin.

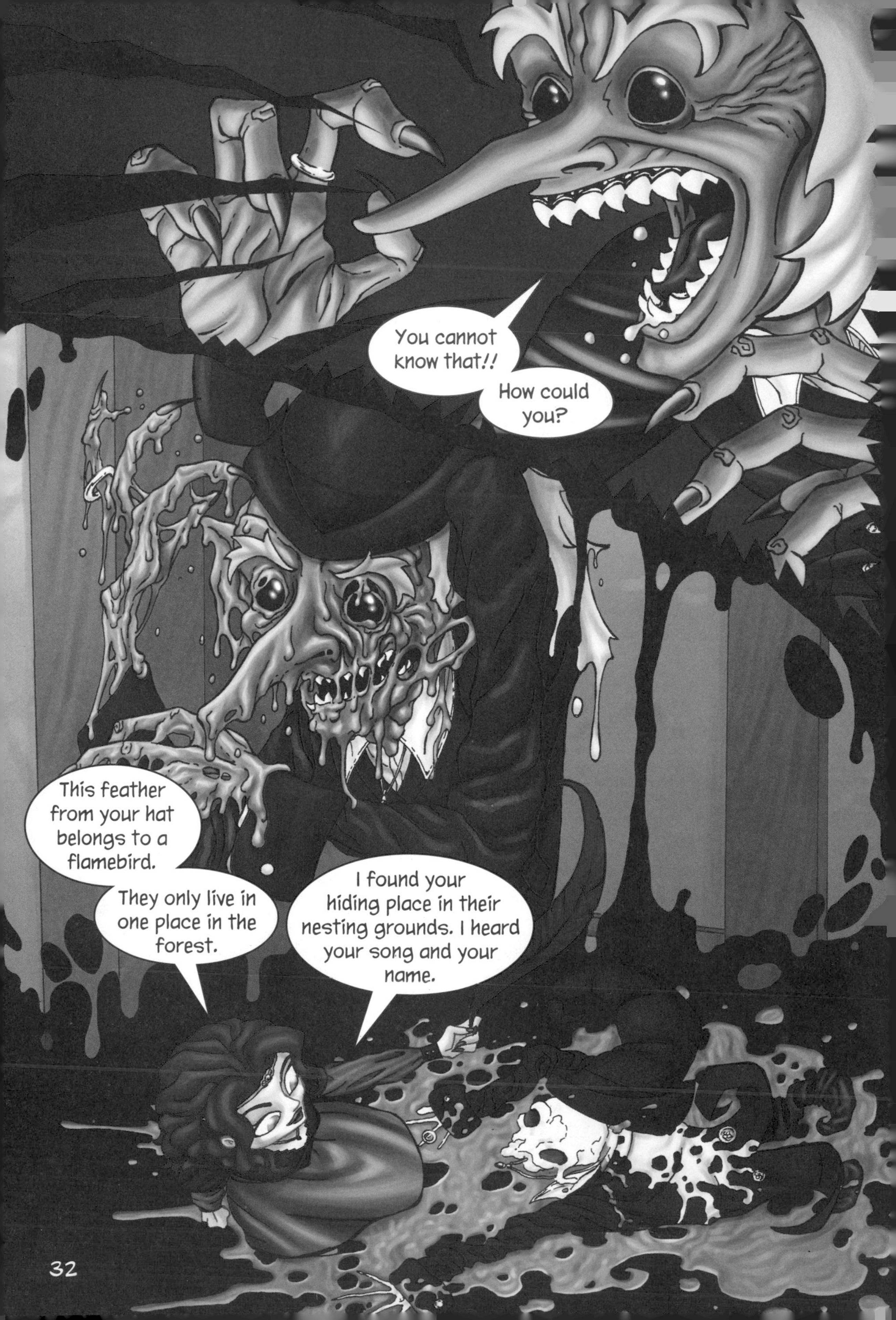
You cannot know that!!
How could you?
This feather from your hat belongs to a flamebird.
They only live in one place in the forest.
I found your hiding place in their nesting grounds. I heard your song and your name.

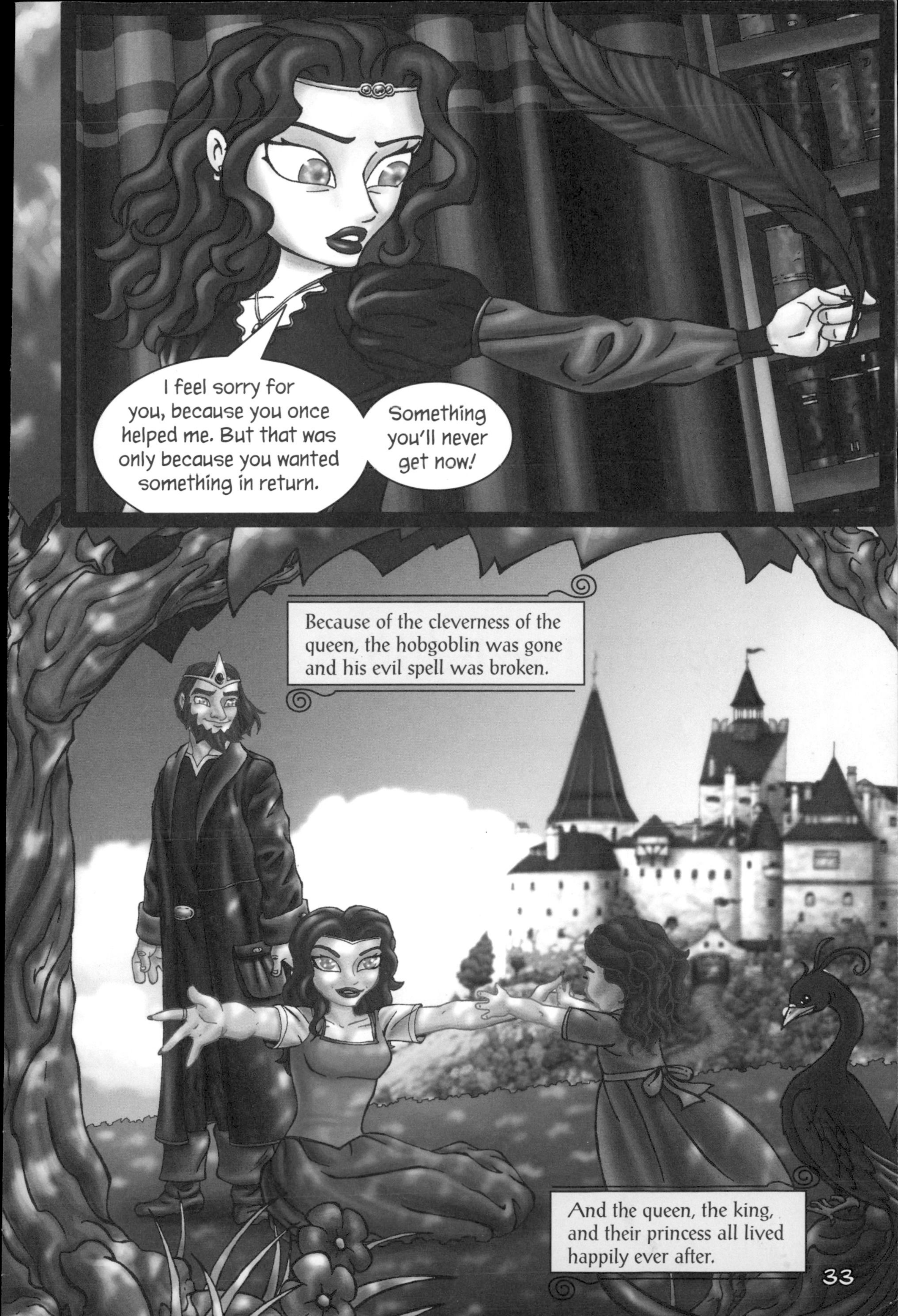
I feel sorry for you, because you once helped me. But that was only because you wanted something in return.
Something you'll never get now!
Because of the cleverness of the queen, the hobgoblin was gone and his evil spell was broken.
And the queen, the king, and their princess all lived happily ever after.

ABOUT THE AUTHOR

Since 1986, Martin Powell has been a freelance writer. He has written hundreds of stories, many of which have been published by Disney, Marvel, Tekno Comix, Moonstone Books, and others. In 1989, Powell received an Eisner Award nomination for his graphic novel *Scarlet in Gaslight*. This award is one of the highest comic book honors.

ABOUT THE ILLUSTRATOR

Erik Valdez Y Alanis was born and raised in Mexico City, Mexico, and has been drawing since age 2. He uses his passion for art to illustrate, paint, and design. Valdez has won a number of awards for his art including the L. Ron Hubbard Gold Award for Illustrator of the Future in 2004. He has done illustrations for books, magazines, and CD covers. Today, Valdez has focused on comics including, most recently, *The Sleepy Truth* for Viper Comics. When he's not working, Valdez loves traveling, really good books, and chocolate cake.

GLOSSARY

bargain (BAR-guhn)—something that is bought for less money than it is worth

behold (bi-HOHLD)—to look at something with great interest

dame (DAYM)—a formal title for a woman

debt (DET)—an amount of money or something that you owe

disappoint (diss-uh-POINT)—to let someone down by failing to do what he or she expected

flamebird (FLAYM-burd)—a mythical bird

highness (HYE-ness)—a title given to members of a royal family

hobgoblin (HOB-gob-lin)—a mythical creature

miller (MIL-ur)—a person who owns or operates a mill

miracle (MEER-uh-kuhl)—an amazing event that cannot be explained

punishment (PUHN-ish-ment)—to make someone suffer for a crime they committed

sire (SYER)—a formal title for a man

spell (SPEL)—a word or words supposed to have magical powers

THE HISTORY OF RUMPELSTILTSKIN

Rumpelstiltskin has been around for hundreds of years. Like most classic fairy tales, the story was passed down orally from one generation to the next. As early as the 16th century, the evil hobgoblin and his magical powers were known throughout Europe. In 1577, the character made his first appearance in a German book called *Geschichtenklitterung or Gargantua* by author Johann Fischart.

Historians and scholars disagree on where the name Rumpelstiltskin comes from. Some believe the name comes from the German word *Rumpelstilzchen*, which means "little rattle stilt," or a creature that rattles posts. Others believe the name is more closely related to *Rumpelgeist*, a goblin-like monster.

No matter what the name's meaning, the story of Rumpelstiltskin remains the same. In fact, in many different countries, the goblin is not named Rumpelstiltskin at all. In Ireland, the little creature is known as Trit-a-Trot, and in Scotland he is known as Whuppity Stoorie.

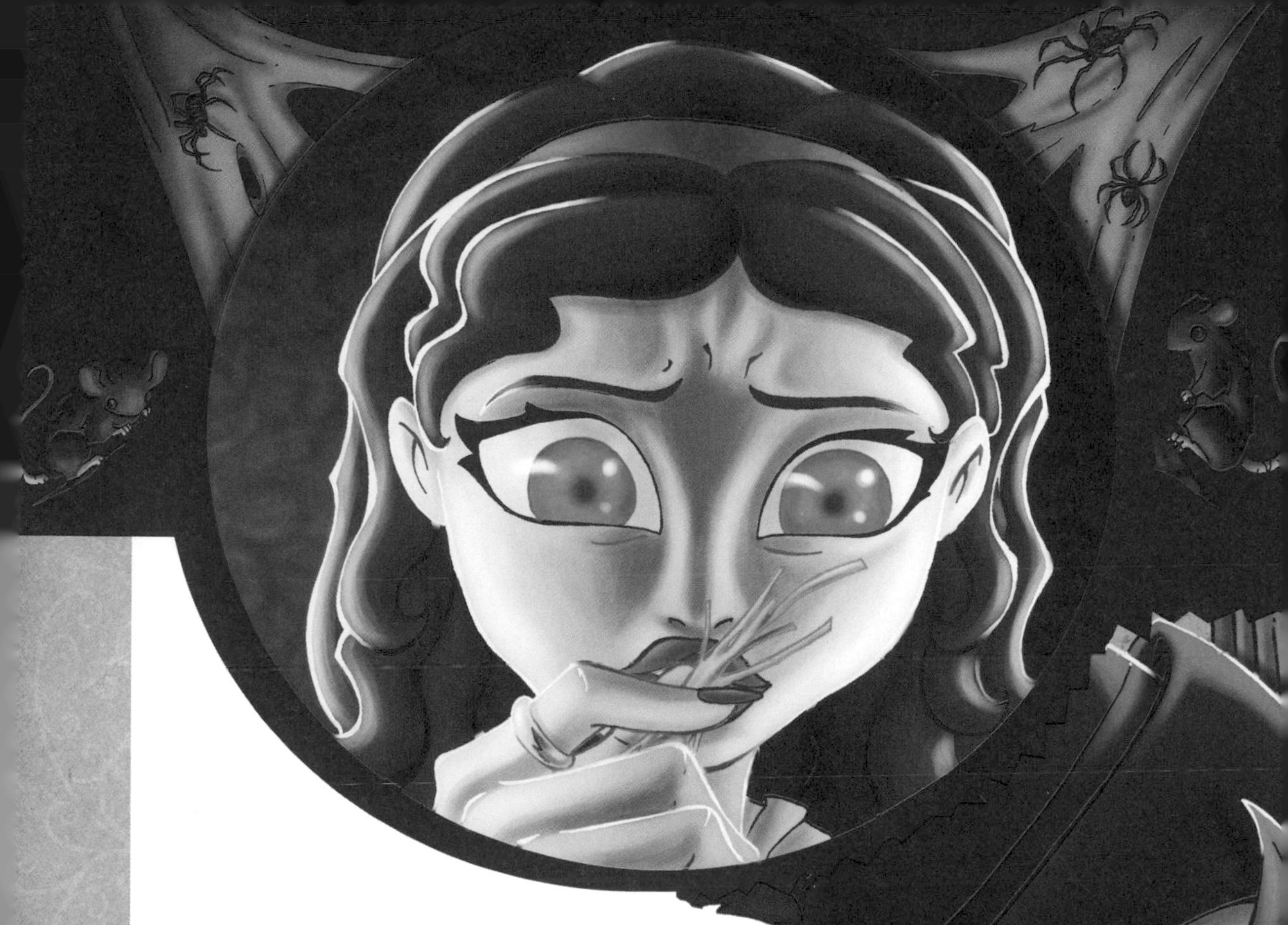

The best-known version of the **Rumpelstiltskin** fairy tale comes from Jacob and Wilhelm Grimm. The brothers traveled around Europe collecting many of the greatest folktales ever told, including "Cinderella," "Rapunzel," and "Hansel and Gretel." In 1812, they published their book of collected stories called *Children's and Household Tales.* Today, this book is known as *Grimm's Fairy Tales* and is still enjoyed by children around the world.

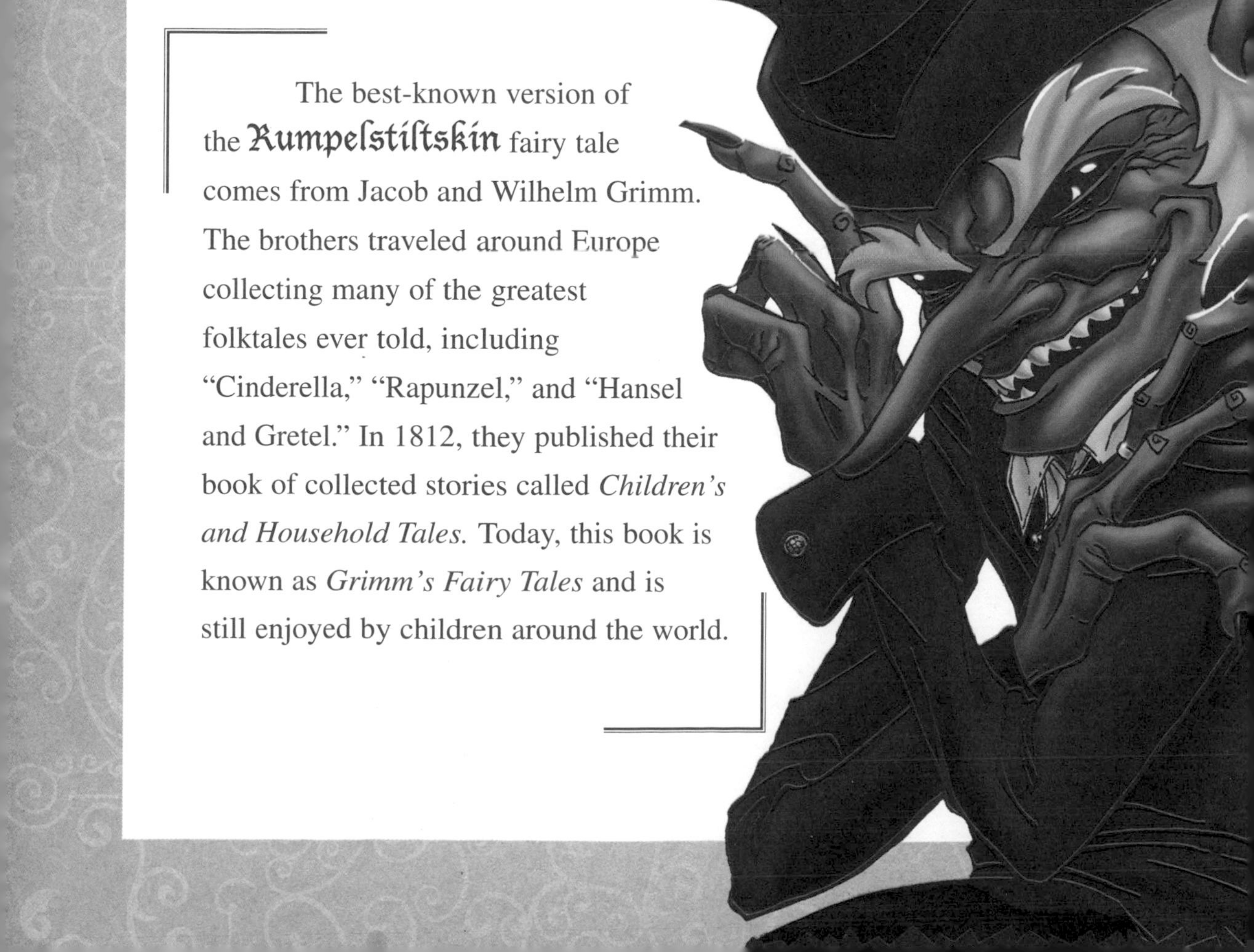

DISCUSSION QUESTIONS

1. Do you think Mirabelle should have accepted the help of Rumpelstiltskin? Why or why not? What could she have done instead?

2. Do you think King Konrad was a good or evil king? Do you think Mirabelle should have married him? Explain your answers.

3. Fairy tales are often told over and over again. Have you heard the Rumpelstiltskin fairy tale before? How is this version of the story different from other versions you've heard, seen, or read?

WRITING PROMPTS

1. Fairy tales are fantasy stories, often about wizards, goblins, giants, and fairies. Many fairy tales have a happy ending. Write your own fairy tale. Then, read it to a friend or family member.

2. Imagine you have the power to turn straw into gold. What would you do with all the money? Write a short story about how you would spend it.

3. At the end of the story, the author says Mirabelle and King Konrad lived happily ever after. What do you think happened next? Will Rumpelstiltskin ever return? Will Mirabelle forgive her father? Use your imagination and write a second part to the story.

INTERNET SITES

The book may be over, but the adventure is just beginning.

Do you want to read more about the subjects or ideas in this book? Want to play cool games or watch videos about the authors who write these books? Then go to FactHound. At www.facthound.com, you'll be able to do all that, and more. The FactHound website can also send you to other safe Internet sites.

CHECK IT OUT!